FATE'S BITE SERIES

GABRIELLA

ELENA M. REYES

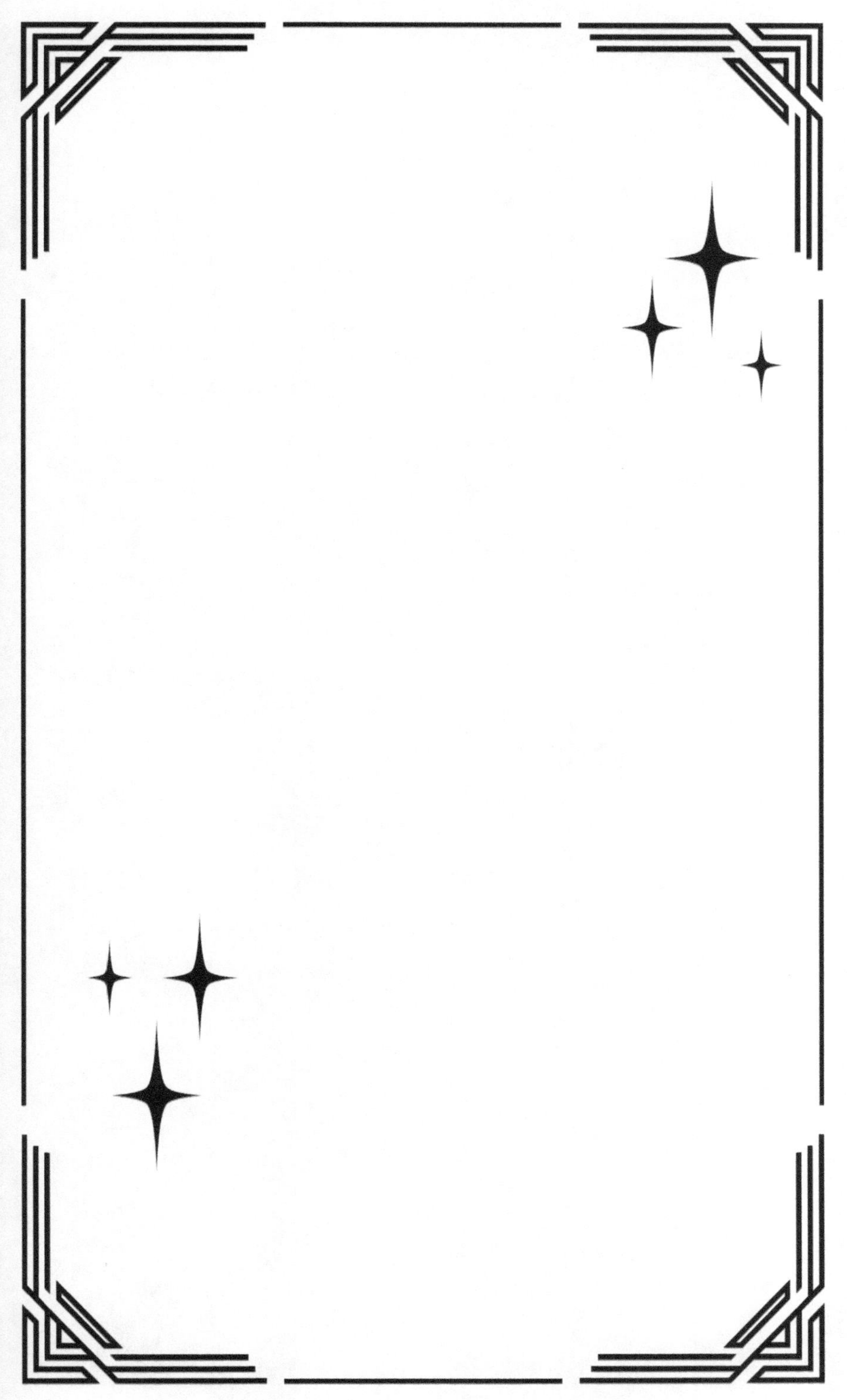

SUMMARY:

*There's no one above a **KING...***

And yet, I'm restless.

I'm an uncontrollable beast that throbs in time with the heartbeat lulling me closer while a sweet, feminine scent overtakes my senses. I've never felt this before—a hunger so frenzied that I'm lost to its call. This siren's song is solely meant for me, and I give in without pause or question.

Because I know and accept.

A single drop of blood running through her veins is worth more than every soul walking this earth. She is now what tethers me to this world.

And the second I see her face, I'm done for. Nothing fucking matters.

I AM DARKNESS.

I AM SIN.
I AM YOURS.

I'll live and breathe for my Queen. My *pretty girl*.

Check out the Spotify Playlist for LITTLE MATE.
Each song has been my faithful companion while I write
this dark and delicious VAMPIRE romance.

LITTLE
MATE
Playlist

LITTLE MATE (Fate's Bite #2)
was written by Elena M. Reyes
Copyright 2021 ©Elena M. Reyes

Cover Design: T.E. Black

Editor: Marti Lynch

Publication Date: Dec 6th, 2021
Genre: FICTION/Dark Romance/Erotica Suspense/Thriller
Copyright © 2021 Elena M. Reyes

ACKNOWLEDGMENTS

This one's for the girls that love their books dark, crazy AF, and the heroes a little dirty. Theo wasn't done and I'm so excited for you to read how it all began.

HAPPY READING, MY BEAUTIFUL BABES!!!

Also, a huge THANK YOU to my team.
Seriously, I couldn't do this without you.

Michelle Myers, Ana Rita, C.M. Steele, Marti Lynch, & Tonya Fox Summerlin; you guys don't let me throw in the towel or doubt myself. You push. Love. Encourage. This book is finished because each of you never let me quit.

I love you all so much and I'm thankful to have you in my life.

Also, another HUGE thanks to Lyra Parish and her kick-ass sprints. Those things are heaven-sent and so much fun!!!

XOXO

Vampire King
THEODORE ASTOR

PROLOGUE

"My Lord, we have word from Naples." My head snaps toward the man who spoke, a lowly guard who cowers under my stare while the stench of fear permeates the air around us. It's strong; the scent coming from him overtakes nature's fragrance as we pause not far from my castle's doors.

"Speak."

He swallows hard. "The siblings are back on Italian soil."

"Are you sure?" I ask, my tone hard, and he nods, body visibly flinching—stumbling back. However, the low warning hiss from me makes him freeze and I take a step closer, my now red eyes daring him to move again. "Use your words."

He's aware of my every step, yet the need to submit to his king forces his head down. His focus is on the ground near my feet. "Yes, sir. All three of the Moore children have arrived as you predicted."

"Guards?"

"Three with them at the moment."

"Hmmm." Taking my eyes off his pathetic form, I look up toward the early morning sky. The sun's rising fast, the warm rays blanketing the land and killing the last remnants of a wet, stormy night. Its dominance is admirable, a little volatile in its unforgiving nature as leaves begin to dry and the temperature rises, causing many to seek refuge indoors.

The vampire cowering in my presence whines a bit, and I smirk in amusement.

My children can't stand the sun's rays for long.

It depletes their strength before turning them to ash if no cover is found.

They thrive in the shadows. It's why they hunt at night while I walk amongst the living.

"Good." I don't say anything else and turn, heading home for the first time in the last two weeks. The rest of my men have dispersed and gone home, while another battalion awaits my orders, and this man will head back to the post that he watches.

A chain connection where my eyes track those who have caught my attention.

Moreover, I know she'll come to me. I've left enough clues, and if Gabriella is anything like her father, anger will override common sense, and that's something I'm counting on.

That ire will be her downfall.

Crossing the bridge that leads to my home, I pause and tilt my head to the side. "Something is off." I can sense it, and my feet carry me toward the large ornate doors while those standing watch immediately remove themselves from my line of sight. There's a change in me the moment I step inside the castle, an overwhelming hunger that pulls a deep rumble from my chest as an intoxicating scent infiltrates my senses.

It's sweet—so fucking alluring—and I follow it to my private wing.

Every vampire in the palace has made themselves scarce; I can still hear the whimpers of many as they run from me, the scared sound only fueling the dangerous need rising within my throbbing veins. My warning growls are low, building inside my chest while my lips curl up to expose my elongated fangs still lightly coated in blood from my last meal.

And they are completely right to run.

The volatile emotions rushing through me will blind my senses; jealousy is an unpredictable emotion.

I inhale again, running the tip of my tongue across my teeth, and groan. "Mate."

Her scent is strong here; I can almost physically feel her in the air around me.

So close. My body thrums with the need to simply touch this stranger. This woman, whose sole existence robs me of rationality while the urge to dig my teeth into her neck and gift her the markings that will adorn her flesh for the rest of our eternal lives, slams into me with the force of a battering ram.

She's not a vampire. She smells of sin.

My body thrums, pleasure coursing through my limbs as another deep inhale infiltrates my senses. I can almost taste her on my tongue while my mate's scent gives me more satisfaction than every drop of blood I've consumed since my birth.

I'm going to enjoy changing her. Feeding on her while she tightens on my cock.

I need my scent to embed deep, to meld with her very essence, almost more than I crave her blood. Because the moment I mark her, to everyone she will smell of me. Of this man—beast—that will kill without remorse if anyone comes near his queen. Every muscle in my body—every single molecule in my vampiric DNA —accepts her, and I don't pause until I'm outside my bedroom door.

It's then that I make out her heartbeat. This *thump, thump, thump* lulls me into a state of serenity I've never experienced before. That I don't know how to feel about. It's confusing yet intriguing, and I'm hungry for a taste of the woman responsible.

"Motherfuck," I hiss out, rubbing a hand over my thick cock while pressing down hard enough to alleviate the uncontrollable need to mount her, but it only serves to make it worse. So much fucking worse when I hear her take in a deep breath of her own, pulling me into her small lungs and letting out a breathy sigh.

Such a sweet little sound. So perfect.

Then, there's the shift in my mattress, the small rustling of sheets I can hear, and I'm barging in without a second thought. The door slams against the wall; her plump mouth lets out a squeak and head turns in my direction.

The second I see her face, I'm done for. Nothing fucking matters.

I'll live and breathe for my pretty girl.

Vampire King THEODORE ASTOR

"You're far from the protection of your forest, old friend," I say, feeling a large presence fill the inside of my office, his aura too huge to contain. Looking up from the paper I was reading, I sit back and meet his green eyes. "Come for a drink, or…?"

"You're older than me, Theodore."

"And yet, I could pass for your son."

His chuckle is dry, posture stiff. "Not true. My children are all under twenty-one summers."

I arch a brow, but my lips curl up a bit at the corner. "Why are you here, Paolo? Are you hiding from Leonora?"

"No." He shifts, hands gripping the back of the chair across from my desk. "She sent me here."

"Why?"

"I need your help, Theodore."

This isn't the proud man I know. He's not one for unannounced visits or drawing out conversation.

Then, there's the scent of death surrounding him. It's harsh, almost sulfur-like in its earthy yet acrid fragrance that cloaks those who are ready to pass.

Vampires can sense this.

It distinguishes a fresh food source from the old and unappetizing. All beasts—animals—have this sixth sense tattooed into their DNA.

We enjoy the kill. The chase. Fresh blood.

Leaning back in my seat, I tilt my head to the side while waving a hand toward the chair he's gripping. The invitation is there, and he takes it while I appraise his every move. Something smells foul. "Speak."

"You smell it?" The warlock king sighs, scrubbing a heavy hand down his face at my nod. "I've done what I can, so my people don't sense it, but it grows nearer. Fate is a cruel mistress and unavoidable. What's written in the book of life must be."

"You've seen it?"

"I have. Si." Paolo taps two fingers against his forehead. Much like one of his twin daughters, the man has the gift of sight. His clairvoyance is subjective to touch and the paths presented, while hers comes freely, a gift with use but not one that entices me. The other one, though... "The time draws near."

"And the rest of your family?" At my question, Paolo produces a set of scrolls and a sealed letter from the right pocket of his long black robe. The hood's down, and his shoulder-length salt-and-pepper hair hangs limply. "What's this?"

"I come asking for a favor, Theodore."

"You know my help comes at a cost."

"I'm willing to risk anything to protect those I love."

"Then ask, my friend. What do you need from me?" Lifting the golden goblet to my right, I bring it to my lips and take a long sip. The rich taste of the blood settles on my tongue; the donor was an adult human male from a nearby village who trespassed on my grounds while hunting for wild game. It's earthy, the coppery tang sustaining me, but doesn't quell the burning need inside of me that grows daily.

Nothing does. Hasn't for a very long time.

Paolo lets out a harsh breath then, yet extends one hand to me. I expect this.

A reassurance that I'll agree before he speaks, but I don't take it. Something he accepts.

His hand remains in the air between us but relaxes a bit. "There's a small cluster of covens that live out on the border of our land that seeks my head. They're planning to rise against me—us—and dismember each ruling house. These people are extremists—an anti-monarch group who's teamed up to strike against Leonora and me within the next full moon."

"So kill them and be done with it." I see no problem. No need to accept fate.

"I wish it was that simple," he spits out, fingers clenching and releasing, yet his hand remains held out. "I'd be displaying their heads embedded on a stake outside my door if it were. Making an example out of them would be a pleasure."

"Then?"

"They have others aiding their cause."

"Others?"

"Yes. The Mariano and Rossi families have betrayed me, yet they're not the biggest threat." His eyes close, nose scrunching up as if smelling something rancid, and yet all scents inside my domain remain the same. All except the slow decay coming from his very pores. "Their allies' magic is dark, Theodore. More depraved than anything I've encountered in all my years walking the earth. It's suffocating."

"Outside your jurisdiction?"

"Yes."

"There are only two other species who work with magic, Paolo."

"The fae or merfolk."

"Both are dangerous…" I say, taking a hearty drink "…yet they don't work well with others. Wouldn't be hard to pick them apart." Another sip. My mind's going through possibilities—motives—and each is greedy enough to try and make a move. "They're too hot-headed and self-righteous to trust anyone's competence. I don't see the connection between them and those smaller covens you speak of, but I'm interested. What do you seek?"

"I've seen it."

"I believe you." He wouldn't lie to me. I'd kill him without hesitation. "But more importantly, is it my support or my army that you need?"

Paolo swallows hard. For a second, his hand falters, still suspended mid-air, but Moore rights it and holds firm. "I need you to protect her at all costs, Theodore. No matter what. No matter how. Gabriella must come first."

"Just her?" That's the first question that comes to mind, but not the first thought. What he's offering is dangerous for her, but very enticing for me. "You have two other kids and a wife—"

"Leonora and I, we won't make it." His scent magnifies, death and sadness surrounding him. "Our fate is sealed."

"I'm sorry."

"It is what it is, but my daughter needs protection." With his other hand, he pushes the scrolls and the sealed letter closer. "Gabriella's special—coveted. Her ability to take and give life scare most, while those seeking power or to expand their territory want to claim her as a mate. She'll never allow that, and I worry that she'll be—"

"Killed," I say, finishing for him. Not that I'd let that happen. It doesn't sit well with me for some reason. I'm a bastard, know and accept it, and I'd also never allow anyone to own—control—her powers, other than myself.

Paolo nods, pain radiating across his features. "Please protect her."

"Why not have her save you?" I'm curious about this. Is she as powerful as he says? For years, his daughters have been rumored to be both beautiful and untouchable. Many have made plans, tried to befriend the man sitting across from me begging for help—to get close to the twins—and yet none have succeeded in so much as meeting them. They're kept away from those outside of his people. Those who live on Moore's sacred grounds. "She could save you, no?"

"If she interferes, she dies. Isabella has seen this."

"Your other daughter?"

"Si."

My eyes narrow. Something isn't adding up. "What aren't you telling me? Why not bring her with you?"

"Because it's not time yet."

"Time for what?" I hiss out, my fangs dropping in a show of annoyance. Riddles and half-truths are the wrong approach when asking me for a favor. "Be honest, or get out."

"My Gabriella is too smart for that, Theodore. Bringing her here or involving her in any way will be a death sentence."

"You're not making sense."

"I know." He leans over, begging me with his eyes to take his hand. To trust him. "Leonora and I have chosen to protect them the only way we can, Theodore. Our three children have different routes they must take, all separate from the other, and you are Gabriella's. You'll understand why when destiny places her in your path. She will be of great importance to your kingdom: her place is here."

"And her power?" His offer can be lucrative for me. Presents a very delicious opportunity.

"She will comply. I've left instructions in the letter atop your desk with my seal."

"Are you sure you don't want to save yourself?" A small part of me does feel bad for the man. To know your end is near—see it—can't be an easy pill to swallow. I've also known him for a long time.

I consider him a man of honor and an ally. "Fate is what you make it."

"There is no other choice."

"Okay." Taking his hand, I give it a firm squeeze. "I'll protect her, Paolo."

"Thank you."

"Don't thank me yet. My intentions aren't completely innocent."

"They're not, but you'll know soon enough that fate is unavoidable. She will surprise you."

Vampire King
THEODORE ASTOR

"Where is she?" I snarl a few weeks later, fangs breaking through the skin of my bottom lip while each man inside my throne room freezes, eyes downcast. They tremble, my ire infiltrating every inch of my castle and the scurry of feet—each person under my employ leaving the grounds—can be heard as if it were a herd of wild animals escaping the jaws of a predator.

Because I am a beast. A demon.

Their fear is heady. A delicious tease to my senses, and I almost smile at the way each general—two men who are nearly as blood-thirsty as I am—flinch back when I lean forward in my seat. Neither speaks. No one does, while those closest to the back release a low hissing sound of distress.

They're also the first to drop down to one knee in a show of fidelity while placing a closed fist on their chests. The entire room moves in synchronization, a gesture I appreciate but, at the moment, is quite useless.

I made a promise. *I will find you, Gabriella Moore.*

The few beads of drawn blood have begun to dry, and I catch them with a rough slide of my tongue across the now sealed wound. Each drop is small but potent, and the scent of my last meal remains on my skin.

Not that I savor them these days.

Each body I drain is a means to an end. Like the human husband of a witch brought to me by General Veltross, who's the older of the two and a bit pompous but knows his place and is ruthless on the battlefield. The offering, though, was meant to lead me to my prize, but instead, I'm tasked with the destruction of yet another worthless coven.

She's one of the sects Warlock Moore spoke of. The dark revolution is brewing in their world, a group of power-thirsty entities who wish to overthrow their monarchy before moving on to the next...

Witch.

Werewolf.

Fae.

Mer.

Vampire.

And all with the end prize of domination and the subjugation of each species.

It's why Moore came to me. Our deal was simple.

I offer protection, and Gabriella will grant me the use of her gift as I please. She doesn't know about this, our agreement, but I have in my possession his signature and a private letter meant to explain with their family seal as authenticity.

I'm being generous with my attempt to gain her acceptance.

She will be under my rule either way. My new pet.

The witch whimpers then, a pitiful cry leaving the back of her throat, and I look over. Her brown eyes are staring at the almost-perished lump at my feet. He's bleeding from his neck while both arms and his left leg are crushed from my earlier grip. And yet, the man clings to life. Barely. Chest rising ever so slowly, and every being in this room knows his time draws near.

I can end it quickly.

Or I can force her to watch his painful end.

Her mate was cursed the moment she laid eyes on him—when she decided to get in my way—and I'm making her witness his last choked breaths as punishment.

My mercy lies in her ability to be of help.

And like other donors, she will also quench my thirst after, yet fail to satisfy me.

Nobody has over the last few decades.

Moreover, my sole focus is *Gabriella* at the moment. On finding the deceased warlock king's daughter to appease an obligation—my final promise to a friend—while taking possession of someone every asshole alive covets, man and beast. The strong and the weak.

Because we all want the same thing: power.

I also won't deny that her gifts turn me on. Then, there's also my curiosity as a man; the predator in me is enticed by the chase.

I don't know what she looks like. Where she is. But I've been left with a *you'll know* from a man whose sight is unlike anything I've encountered before.

The thought of taming the little witch is a heady aphrodisiac I plan to indulge in. Continuously. Will seduce her without shame.

My need is growing, body thrumming with a fire I don't understand, yet welcome.

An angry hiss leaves the back of my throat then, the sound full of ire while my fangs drop another inch over my bottom lip. I'm close to my edge, ire brimming; it clashes and fuels my lust—this unyielding need to own her.

Their lack of results is something I'll never accept.

At the angry sound, they tense a little more. More than a few lower themselves until their foreheads touch the ground and both arms lay palms flat next to their heads. A request for mercy. For leniency.

These cowering statues won't receive any from me. I survey each, from rank to usefulness until coming to a stop at my two generals. One still holds his head downcast, while the braver of the two turns his face in my direction and meets my eyes.

He disapproves of my quest.

Hates anything outside of our vampiric world.

He's a fucking idiot. His prejudice will be his downfall one day, but until then, I'll continue to use Veltross as the puppet he's become. A mindless killer.

"My Lord, we've—" I cut General Veltross off with a single look in his direction and he recoils, his other leg giving out under the weight of my stare. He has balls, yet not much in the area of perseverance. His rank means shit to me.

No one is above me.

My sharp nails tap against the wooden arm of my throne, the *clink clink clink* loud inside the large room. "Your excuses bore me."

"Please, sire. We are—"

"Not another word. Understood?" Veltross nods, and I turn my face toward the dark witch. She's already in mourning. Her body is wracked with sobs, and yet I feel no remorse. Not when her soul is as black as mine—her end goal is to eradicate the Moore bloodline. "Lilibeth, I'm going to give you one last chance to gain my favor. Where. Is. She?"

"I'll never tell you."

"Is that your final answer?"

"Fuck you."

"No, thank you." Flicking my eyes toward the second general, I snap a finger. "Brodej, are they outside in the training field?"

At once, he acknowledges me with a respectful glance. "Yes, my lord."

"Thank you." Valtross's face grows tight at that, and I direct my attention back to him. Dare him to say a word; he doesn't. "Bring her outside. She seems to need a little fresh air."

"Yes, my lord."

Standing from my seat, I walk down the center of the room toward the door. As I pass each row of soldiers, they begin to stand and then turn their formation to follow my every move.

Without pause, I slam open the room's solid teak doors, ignoring the way they ram into the wall and how some of the golden filigree decoration crumbles under the impact. My steps are loud, and my destination is the back of my castle where her second lesson will commence.

No one is above Theodore Astor. You do not defy me.

The men escorting my guest keep a few feet of distance between us. They're also silent, enjoying the struggles and cries escaping Lilibeth's scared and angry form, the pitiful sounds filling the wide-open space.

It's late in the evening now, the sky overcast, and the scent of rain lingers in the air. It greets us as we enter the large field just behind the castle's rear exit. The rest of my kingdom's troops stand at attention, leaving the area to the left of where I stand empty, but not for long as the heavy footfalls of every vampire who'd been inside the throne room vibrate against the ground.

They take their positions, standing tall and with their eyes straight ahead while I turn my attention to Lilibeth and Brodej.

She's struggling in his hold, thrashing. "Let me go!" He doesn't answer. Instead, he lifts her feet off the ground, both hands gripping her upper arms tightly. "You will regret this. I will curse—"

"Sister, please." That catches her attention. Lilibeth goes from spitting mad to eerily quiet within a single breath. Her eyes focus on the one who spoke. The shock in them is quite a pretty sight.

"Palermo." It's a whisper, the sound full of sorrow. Her head shakes from side to side, her body limp in Brodej's hold while her eyes roam down the line of kneeling men, every ranking member of her smaller coven. All men. Her family. "Oh God, no. No."

"I'll ask you again, Lilibeth." Taking the remaining steps between us, I stand in her line of sight and pull her eyes toward me with the tip of a finger. "Where is Gabriella Moore? Where is she hiding?"

"I can't."

"You will." I hold a hand up, and a scream rends the air. It's male, an older one at that, and Lilibeth's eyes close in misery. The scent of blood is heavy in the air and a few vampires hiss, taking a step forward but no more than that as her father's life essence stains the grass. "That cut across his chest is shallow, my dear. The next won't be as gentle."

"Have you no heart?" she asks, voice low and full of so much pain. "How can you hurt my mate—innocent men? They don't deserve this cruelty."

"Innocent? The man who plunged the stolen Stygian blade deep into his own king's chest? That's who you call innocent?"

"He didn't—"

Ignoring her attempt to save her father's life, I look out toward my army. Men and women who are loyal to me. "Is the man responsible for his queen's torture then decapitation worthy of mercy?"

"No," in unison, they answer.

"Does he deserve death?"

"Yes."

"An eye for an eye?" The soldier holding Lilibeth's kin, a woman who's second-in-command of a battalion under her husband, Brodej, takes heed to my demand, and with her sharp nail digs the orb out of its socket. Her nail is embedded deep, the eye and the attached ligament dangling from her small finger. Once again he screams, the sound pleasurable to my senses. Because a predator enjoys cornered prey—the scent of fear that seeps from their every pore. "Or perhaps a limb? He did molest her, after all."

"Please don't," the man, an older version of Lilibeth's crying brother, pleads. "We can come to an agreement over the sisters. We only want one of them."

"Can we?"

"Father, please—"

"Enough, Daughter. I will not die for that whore." His words anger me. Ire fills my veins—the blood of my victims runs through me—at his blatant disrespect of what I already consider mine. She will be under my protection.

As the first vampire and king, I was born into this life with a few human traits, although there's nothing within my DNA that is alive. I've never been, and yet this gift is one of them. It keeps my temperature warm while my children are cold—unable to fully walk in the light without pain or being drained of all energy.

I feel neither and enjoy the sun.

I need no sleep to rejuvenate.

"They won't kill us if we remain quiet." This comes from the man next to her father. He holds a familial resemblance. "We're their only hope to—"

Before he can blink, I'm in front of him. His horrified expression is amusing a second before his lips drop open, but the sound never leaves them as I rip his head clean off. Blood coats my hands and shirt—the men on either side of him also wear a bit of the crimson liquid.

Taking off the ruined garment, I toss it at the corpse before craning my neck from side to side. A smirk curls at my lips while I run my blood-stained fingertips across my chest and the monarch tattoos that have marked my flesh from the day of my birth. From my pecs to my back, the piece is massive and tells you my about origins and the demon I am.

At the sight, Lilibeth retches behind me, but I pay her no mind. Taking a step toward the next member of her coven, my eyes meet the shaking form of a younger man, a kid of no more than his eighteen summers.

From her father comes a sound of protest, but it stops when the female soldier drags his eyeball, still attached to her nail, down his cheek from the socket to just the corner of his lips. She's waiting for my signal to proceed, but a minute shake of my head has her falling back into a rigid formation.

Shoulders back. Face forward and held high.

Those kneeling from his faction flinch at her sudden movement, but it's the young man in front of me I focus on. "Do you feel safe?"

The lad shakes his head. He trembles. "No, sir."

"So polite." My tone is a bit patronizing, but so is the way I study the drying blood on my skin. "I appreciate the manners."

"Thank you." His grimace right after is amusing.

"Why are you here...?" I trail off, waiting for his name.

"Christopher. My name is Christopher."

"And why are you here, Christopher? How are you involved in this mess?"

"Guilty by association. That was my father you killed." No emotion, though. I sense no sadness in him.

"My condolences." A lie. He knows it, too, but he's wise and remains quiet after. Christopher doesn't meet my eyes now either. Lowering his face, he stares at my boot-covered feet while those around him begin to mutter something in unison.

One by one, the small chant gains momentum while we remain as we are.

No one stops them. No one breaks a jaw to cut off the offending cry.

Louder. And louder.

Revertere ad inferos. Revertere ad inferos. Revertere ad inferos.

Lilibeth isn't participating, though. Instead, her focus is on the body of her lover brought outside by one of my men. The human is tossed to the ground, and his low groan of pain—the last of his energy now depleted—meets her ears and she goes still.

Her eyes roll back. The leaves around us rustle, lift from the ground and swirl around her and the guard keeping her in place.

She's angry. Volatile.

Lightning strikes, but it's nothing more than a soft electrical buzz surrounding my body.

Lilibeth showed her hand; she has an affinity for controlling lightning. A little bit of wind, too, but neither does real damage, which leads me to believe her power is new or she hasn't completely learned how to manipulate it to her liking. Nothing else—nothing but the harsh charge of current that strikes unforgivingly, and while I should've been burned to a crisp right now, her people are not the only ones protected by magic.

I am indestructible. No power nor human-made weapon will ever destroy what I've built.

Mate. Four letters that put together become my sole point of weakness; I'm blessed to not have found her. There is no room in my life for distractions. For frailty.

"Lilibeth, no!" her father screams, but it's too late.

Before they realize what I'm doing, I push Christopher a few feet from the lineup and then I'm standing in front of her, hand around her throat. She gasps, choking as my fingers tighten—lift until those dirty feet float above the ground.

"Let go," she cries out, her fingernails tearing as they fail to break my skin. The bloody tips slip, her body thrashing while I move her into position. Her back is now against my chest, and her sobs vibrate through me. "I'll tell you. Just stop....no!"

Placing my lips against her ear, I exhale against her head. She smells of rosemary and rain, and the scent is wrong. Irritates my senses. "Watch them. You did this."

The man standing behind her brother slides two fingernails across his neck from left to right, and blood pours from the wound. The cut is deep and the man's head falls back only, staying upright because the vampire behind him holds him in place.

The next three die much the same way. Lilibeth's screams rend the wide-open space, and I smirk against her temple. My army is hungry; they hiss and their muscles coil tight as the ground soaks up the blood beneath their feet. They won't feed on them as this entire family is scum—tainted—and the sooner this ends, the sooner I'll find Gabriella.

The next in line is her father.

Pompous. Arrogant. Pathetic.

His complexion is now pallid; the blood loss is quite significant. "Don't tell him anything, Lilibeth. Don't you...*fuck*!" Another gouge, this time to the remaining eye. It hangs from the socket, blood streaking his cheek.

"Your call, Lilibeth." Body shuddering, she tries once again to fight my hold. The wind howls, angrier this time, yet it's uncoordinated and does nothing but flutter around us and sweep my dark hair back. "Tell me where she is, and I'll make it all go away."

"He's lying. Don't," her father begs, his hands now braced on the ground in front of him, fingers digging into the dirt. "We're dead anyway. Don't help him."

"True, but..." Her mate whines then, the wheezing sound pulling her back to the present, and everything stills. He is her weakness. My ace up the proverbial sleeve. "I can help him, Lilibeth. Take away his pain." Walking us forward, I turn her to face him while the bodies of her fallen coven brothers are tossed into a pile where they lay with eyes wide open and mouths agape in horror. "Do you want that?" I whisper. "Do you want it all to end? To meet him again?"

"Yes."

"Then tell me. It's that simple." We ignore the gurgling sound of her father's struggles; I take advantage of how she can't look away from the silly human struggling to live. *Yet he's not the only scent on her.* Flicking my eyes to the guard holding the elder witch, I tilt my head in the direction of the castle. They'll know where to take him.

I'll deal with him privately.

Lilibeth remains inconsolable; her cries are soul-deep, but I feel her resolve seconds later. Take account of the breath where she loses her fight. Gives up. Swallowing back a sob, she exhales roughly and whispers the words I've been longing to hear: "New Forest in England."

I let out a rough exhale against her temple before kissing the skin there. "Good girl." Her neck is supple in my hold, the vein pulsing in time with her rapid breathing. Anxiety. There's no fight in her when I tip her head to the side, nor when I breathe in deep, but the horrified scream following my fangs piercing deep—tearing her throat wide open as I feed—is a beautiful memory I'll treasure.

She's made this a little enjoyable. Her emotions are entertaining if nothing else.

Taking in the last deep pull, I press a tiny kiss to her empty vein before tossing her aside. I kept my promise—her mate's already passed, and she'll meet him if there is such a thing as an afterlife.

I walked her to death's door and over the threshold, however, what she finds on the other side isn't my concern.

A frightening sound reaches my ears a few seconds after, and my head turns toward the source. Christopher is huddled against a tree, his bruised body shaking while the scent of piss emanates from him. *Poor kid.*

"Run, child. I'm allowing you to leave."

"Please don't kill—"

"Run, and don't look back. You have sixty seconds before I change my mind."

And while he takes off, stumbling and trampling a black rose bush, I scratch my jaw. Gabriella and her siblings took off for England. *Smart little thing.* She's put enough space between us to make this chase fun.

The Moore family has lived—thrived—here in Italy, in Foresta di Ferràina to be precise, for over a century. Hours separate both kingdoms, never mixing while acknowledging—respecting—the treaty between both.

It'd be so easy to enslave them: our personal feeding horde.

And she's the key. *Mine.*

"I'm coming for you, little girl."

Gabriella

Another coven. Twenty dead bodies.

They're scattered throughout the sacred grounds an hour from the family's home back in Italy, their bodies decapitated and bled dry—the corpses left for our kind to find. No note. No demands, and yet, I know it's my sister and me they seek.

Just like the last two times.

Just like our father warned it would happen.

"King Astor isn't going to give up," I say under my breath, my eyes scanning the report brought to me by a member of the royal guard. He's traveled for days without respite to bring this, his body needing emergency assistance upon arrival. "How can we stop this mess, Isabella? This can't go on…our people won't survive it."

The names of the fallen are written on our sacred paper, and each one hits me in the chest like a small dagger slicing across the beating organ. I'm bleeding for them. *I've failed them.*

The Salicio clan was a quiet group that for the most part governed themselves and came to the Moore home when a grievance needed an impartial ear. My family—my father—has always been fair that way. No dictatorship. Just laws. Our sole expectation is that you respect nature, each other, and those who are not of Wiccan belief.

No matter the species. We strike to kill only in self-defense.

Fight fair and never out of anger, dear child. Volatile emotions are uncontrollable. They'll kill you from within. My father's words ring in my ears as if he were standing beside me. But he's not. They're *both* gone, and I miss them.

"It's going to get worse, Gabby," Isabella whispers from behind me. Her hand on my shoulder gives a gentle squeeze, and I close my eyes. I've read each line in the report a few times, memorizing each detail while my heart mourns for all those innocent lives lost. "We have to go home. It's the only way."

"Leonardo can't go back. He's our hope for the future, sister." Turning my head, I blink and meet her unwavering stare. Tears brim in my eyes, making her face a tiny bit blurry, but I don't let them fall. She's being honest. Our paths will soon deviate from one another and travel down roads without answers or assurances, but if we are to protect those we love, there is no other choice. "Please tell me you've found a loophole."

"There isn't. I'm sorry." The pain in her tone mimics the agony in my heart.

We're alone, and all because of the greed of men not worth the air they breathe. Our people turned against us and accepted the aid and money of others to ascend to power. They've planned and killed, and now hunt us as if we were nothing but wild game running through the dense forests we travel through. From witches to the fae to vampires, however, the latter wants me for a different reason.

The vampire king intends to use me—bend me to his will—but what's worse is the collateral damage left behind as a reminder that he's close. Waiting. Watching. He's toying with me, and I know the time draws near for us to meet.

He's left me a note in the past. Just one, and it corroborates everything Isabella has warned me about.

More importantly, I can't let this go on.

I want them all dead.

Moreover, I'm ready to end my own life if it means my siblings will be safe.

"Fuck." The pain inside my chest explodes then; the control I've been fighting to maintain shatters and my legs give out. Energy pulses all around me. My hands feel the tethers of those dead and alive who walk the halls outside this room. Some are strong, others faint—those who are destined to die soon are the loudest— and they all clamor for my attention.

And I let them speak.

Their hymn has a low cadence that I hold on to. I let it soothe my fragile soul, breathing in and out while Isabella lowers herself beside me. Her fingers gripping mine, our bodies sway as the scream that's building within me finally releases.

The sound is full of anger and hurt—agonizing—and a few wails can be heard coming from the floor below where a group of older women have been tending to the meals of those who've traveled with us. Pain radiates through the walls, and the stones nearly vibrate as tears fall from my eyes.

I've been holding it in for too long, something that Isabella has been warning me about since the night our parents were killed.

"Gabriella, get up!" I hear someone whisper-yell from above me, their hands shaking me awake. I'd fallen asleep outside again, my hands embedded deep into the earth as nature sang a soft lullaby. Because I can feel it; from the tiniest heartbeat to the gentle breaths each leaf exhales.

However, my nose crinkles then. The harsh scent of smoke greets my senses, and my eyes snap open. "What the?"

"Now, sister. We need to go!" Isabella's frantic tone snaps me into focus; I turn toward her voice and take her in. Her face is ashen, her long white dress dirty while her red hair, the tone a few shades

darker than mine, is in complete disarray. My twin looks like crap. "Please, Gabby. Focus. I need you—"

"Why are you here looking like that?" She's barefoot, shaking, and trying to stand in the way of my view behind her. "Stop fidgeting, Isa. Tell me what's wrong."

"Please forgive me."

"You're not making sense. Did someone harass you?"

My twin shakes her head, tears falling from her eyes. "No."

"Did something happen at home?" A whimper leaves her, the sound so full of sorrow. "It had to be this way."

Before she finishes, I'm standing. My eyes dart around, my hands pushing her out of my way so I can see past the tree line that leads to a small ravine at the back of the family home. Smoke billows above the foliage and a sinking feeling settles in my chest, the sharp tendrils of a last breath being exhaled shaking me to the core.

I know that presence.

"Tell me I'm wrong." Reaching out, I grip the front of her dress and pull her closer. My head turns, and blue eyes meet my green ones. So much sorrow. So much guilt. "Where are they?"

"We've been attacked," she says, voice breaking at the end. Her entire small frame shakes. "Dad sent me and Leo out through the tunnels. We made it out before they breached his office."

"Who?"

"The Rossi."

"Lilibeth's family?" A girl I grew up with. One of my closest friends; she's spent days in our house and ate with my parents. We were taught about our history in the same school. We learned about our distinct abilities from the same oracle—my nonna—when we were kids. And years later, when she met her mate, I blessed her union to a human when her father made his disappointment known. "That can't be right. She—they'd never..."

"I'm sorry, Gabby. It had to be this way." Betrayal stings, my stomach churning, but that quickly turns into ire, and I step back. Fire races through my veins before I'm done taking in my next

inhale, her words settling deep. "Dad wouldn't let me intervene. He forbade it."

"You knew." Not a question. The timbre of my voice is dark, harsh, as a veil of black overcasts my senses. "You fucking knew."

"Everyone did, but you and Leo."

"Why?" Isabella raises a hand, asking me to take it, but I won't. I don't want to share our energy or feelings through touch. Let them fester right now. Eat away at my soul that turns black, decays as pain rattles my bones. No. Not now. "Answer me, Isa. Why the hell would you hide this from me?"

"Because you couldn't save him without dying, sister. And his last wish as king was for his children to save his people. We are what's left."

"And Mom? I didn't feel her—"

She closes her eyes. Hides her shame. "They took her."

I'm going to kill them all. Drain their essence and feed it to the earth. *"Where's Leo?"*

"Hidden inside our tree."

Walking past her, I head toward the hiding spot we've kept secret from everyone except those with familial ties. A large, sixty-year-old hollow oak stands a few feet inside the Moore property line; the inside is spacious and easily fits three, and the entrance is high enough to block the sight of those within.

Her steps fall in line with mine a few seconds later. Her anxiety mirrors my own. She's wondering if I'll forgive her, and I will, but not today. "First, we need our little brother safe, and then I need every detail, Isabella. No more secrets."

"Yes."

"We also need to find Mom."

"We might not, and when the time comes, don't hold back. I need you to embrace the pain; the outcome will be horrific if you don't."

"You've seen this, or—"

"Her destiny has always been intertwined with Dad. They will meet again."

"Let it out. Just let yourself feel." Isabella's pain intertwines with mine, and everything around me darkens. The room feels as though it's caving in on us. My throat feels hoarse, her energy feeding off mine as turbulent emotions ravage my soul.

I'm still hurting. I'm angry. I focus on the last tendrils of our parents' spirits who linger near, something my siblings aren't aware of. Our loved ones can't find rest, their souls clamoring for peace, but the feeling of worry seems to dominate that small tether licking at my senses.

It's not unfounded, and the future is uncertain: ours and those we are meant to lead, while so many want us dead.

"We got you, Gabriella," my brother's voice comes from my other side, and I look over, meeting the eyes of a younger version of our father. The resemblance is strong; the sole difference outside of the age is Leo's blue eyes, which he shares with Isa and Mom. From the thick brows to his stubbornness, the kid is a constant reminder and the heir to the Moore throne. "Just cry. You've been strong long enough."

His words bring forth guilt. The last thing he should be worried about is my emotional state.

Leonardo has so much on his shoulders. Too much.

His life thus far has been a nonstop grooming session.

Isabella and me, we'll eventually find our mates, and there's always the possibility that they're not of magical proclivities. They can be anything. Even human. And while we'll help and take control until he comes of age to take the crown, my sister has always made it known that someday, we'd leave.

My sobs quiet down. I fight them back, but the slow roll of tears doesn't abate. Instead, they stain the skirt of my dress, my body hunching over as I breathe deeply in and out, slowly trying to recover my composure. It's a pointless struggle, impossible, because the two people in the world whom I love more than my own life are also struggling.

That's the part of my gift that can be both a blessing and a curse.

To manipulate life, you must open yourself and accept every single part of a person's essence—meld yourself with it. It leaves me susceptible. Empathetic.

"I'm okay," I say after a while. My throat is sore, and swallowing is a bit hard around the still-present knot, but I manage and stand with shaky legs. They follow me, each with a hand gripping my arm. "But we do need to talk. There's a decision to be made, and it affects us all."

"There isn't a choice, Gabby." Leo's expression, while sad, is determined. His inner strength, the warlock within him, demands respect.

This amuses me; a slight chuckle slips past my lips. "Put away the commanding voice, kid. You're not king yet."

"I don't know..." Isabella bumps her shoulder with mine, a smirk on her lips "...this time I agree with his majesty. My lord does know best."

"You two are impossible." His grumble, that thirteen-year-old grumpy demeanor cuts through what's left of my tension. He's not as strong as Isabella and me. His magic hasn't shown signs of surpassing what we experience—feel, see, or manipulate—but he will.

One day.

He's destined for greatness.

"I'm not against going back—"

"But you need to protect me?" Leo cuts in. He's pensive for a few minutes, not meeting my stare but focusing on the wall behind me. Then he paces, turns around, and walks the circumference of the room a few times before coming to a stop in front of us once again with his hands clasped behind his back. *So much like Dad.* "What if I stay with Uncle Roberto? That's close enough, but not in the way. You can reach me quickly if needed while doing what you must to end those responsible."

At the mention of my father's brother, I bite back the curse words sitting on the tip of my tongue. In the two months since our parents' murders, the man never sent word or offered his assistance during our mourning. Never asked if we needed him—or anything—and it doesn't sit well with my soul.

And while I get that he too lost someone he loves, even a hello via the soldiers that took turns and traveled through this city he lives in, the group of three who rotate duties so we'd always have guards, would've meant a lot. I'd know we aren't fully alone. That someone cares.

Think rationally, Gabriella. Emotions don't solve problems, but rather create them.

Dad's words, the ones he's been drilling into my head since my early teens, filter through and I pause. He's right. My personal feelings aside, Leo staying behind and safe is what matters most, and if I must play nice until this all passes, then so be it.

I *will* hash this out with our uncle afterward.

"I'm agreeable to that." Wiping away the last of my tears, I take the few steps between us and hug him, one that Isabella joins while also giving me a nod. Telling me without words that she's on board with this plan. For a few minutes, we remain this way, quietly accepting what's to come and the bloodshed that will follow. *Those who rose against us will die.* "We pack tonight and head out in the morning?"

It's our brother's turn to nod while Isabella lifts her head and meets my red-rimmed eyes. Her expression matches my tumultuous emotions: anger, pain, and sadness. "Let's go home. We can't escape destiny."

Gabriella

Our trip back to Italy has been somber for the most part. Quiet.

The only sound inside the quiet cab of the train we're taking home is that of Leo's snores while Isabella stares out the window. We've been on the move for a few days now; some by water and now by a locomotive, but soon we'll reach Naples where a few of Father's horses await us.

The Salernitano breed is a strong one. It can withstand an enchantment and live longer than the average stallion and travel far without pause. They'll be how we move away from the city—human dwellings—and back into our beloved forest near Messina.

Onyx is my favorite of the three being taken care of by a coven loyal to the crown until our return. They're a little out of the way, but if my father trusted them, then so do we. That, and it was through their help that we reached the boat traveling to England and boarded safely.

Our uncle didn't help. The port closest to us was also being watched.

That longer route gave us the cover we needed.

The screeching of brakes pulls my attention to the present, and I nudge Leo's shoulder. He wakes up, alarmed, sitting up quickly and eyes darting around. Once he sees we're not in danger, my brother relaxes a bit and yawns. "We're here."

"We are, drools." He glares at my jab but wipes his mouth with the sleeve of his shirt. *Gross.* "Isa grabbed some wet towels earlier. They're in the basin next to the door. Clean up a bit."

"Are we having breakfast, or fetching the horses?"

"Breakfast first. We have a long day of travel up ahead," Isa answers for me, her tone tense. Not that our brother catches this, the last dredges of sleep making him unable to notice the glassiness in her eyes and twitch of her hands. She's seeing something. "Please be ready in ten."

Before she's done, he's already swiping the cool cloth across his face and then neck. And knowing his attention is occupied, I turn to look closer at my sister. She's watching me too, her lips stretched into a thin line while that barely perceptible nod sits like lead in my stomach.

One nod: bad news.

Two nods: clear passage.

Motioning with my head at the door, I exit and walk toward the back where there's an empty caboose with a glass windowpane door. It's large enough for us to look through, the door to our cabin not far and accessible.

Isa doesn't make me wait long, and before the door closes behind me, she's stepping through.

We stand side by side, both looking out onto the vast landscape and busy city to the left of the train tracks.

"What is it?"

"We're walking into a bloodbath." A harsh shiver runs through her, the grip she has on the railing turning her knuckles white. "The vampires are getting closer."

"There's something else, isn't there?"

"My sight is being shielded, but yes. Your path is intertwined with his, Gabby."

At her response, I choke out a gasp. *This is bad.* "How can this be?"

"Which one?"

"Both."

Isa shrugs, but I'm not buying the nonchalance. Her worry is palpable. "My guess is a powerful witch, but not stronger than the Moore bloodline. I'll break whatever they've cast."

Nodding, I mull that over. With so many coming for our heads, it'd be easy to have someone help him. "What's his plan, though? Why does the king of vampires need a sorceress?"

"Sadly, you'll ask him personally soon enough."

Fuck. "How much of a window, sister? Do we have time to get Leo to Uncle Roberto's?"

"Three moons."

"Are you sure?" This doesn't leave us much room. I'll barely be back home in that timeframe. "You just said you can't see as clear—"

"The path might change, but the destination doesn't. Fate is a determined bitch."

"She is." *She led us here again.*

"We're safe for now but must move fast." Turning to look behind her, she watches the door of our cabin. "Uncle Roberto is not far from here, just a short coach ride, and we'll stay until late evening to rest. I don't know when we'll see Leo after this, Gabby. The future is blurry; I see a lot of red, but the paths haven't deviated."

"I trust you."

"Thank you."

Squeezing her shoulder, I turn and face the same door as her. "We can't tell him any of this. Not yet."

"Agreed."

"And no hiding anything from the other. We face them all together."

"I'll never purposely keep something from you again."

"Purposely?" I ask, flicking my eyes in her direction. She's already looking at me. "Mind explaining that one?"

"Sister, I can't hide what I don't see." Her statement is simple, but I get it. All magic is susceptible to corruption—all except mine. The god of death doesn't allow interference nor deceit. He's not a merciful being, and neither are those closest to him.

Death has many faces.

The taker. The collector. The keeper.

You steal from one, and hell will rain down on your head.

"By blood and pact," I say, extending a hand out for her to hold. Our fingers intertwine, grip tight, and I feel her emotions—experience the wariness in her soul. "We are one."

"We are one."

———

"Welcome, children. You must be exhausted," Uncle Roberto greets us at the door of his home in the city a few hours later. After getting off the train, we stopped to eat at a small café serving those exiting the station. It wasn't much, a few croissants with coffee and milk, but it held us over while walking toward the center of Naples where he stands with his long robe overshadowing his thin frame. His resemblance to our father is minimal; all they share is the same height, hair color, and the one mole just below his left eye. He's also a non-practitioner. No magic, but a great teacher. "Please, come in."

The guards look over at me and I nod, giving them the okay to resume our preparations; one will stand guard at the front while the other two grab our horses after a small break. They need the respite just as much, and the road ahead is uncertain.

We have to leave today; there's too much to do to delay this any longer.

Our uncle watches the exchange silently, but I see the questions in his eyes. Not that we plan to give him answers, and instead, Isa and I pass him after a quick kiss to the cheek. Leo, however, is another story. His attention is already on the delicious scent of food coming from deeper in the large home.

"Where is she?"

"Silla's in the kitchen, kid." His chuckle is loud. A bit forced. There's also tension around his eyes—a slight rigidness in his posture. "She's been cooking all day...said we'd have visitors today."

"Guess she was right."

If he senses any reproach in my tone, our uncle hides it, keeping his attention on Leo. "Go on..." his head tilts in the direction of the kitchen "...go surprise her."

Leo, though, looks back at us and waits until we nod. The kid's smart. Knows more than people think. "I'll be back."

"Go stuff your face, but if she made bombolone, back off."

Rubbing his hands like a villain, he begins walking backward toward our aunt and food. "I make no promises. Sweets before salty."

"Try me." Taking a threatening step toward him, the kid turns and runs. His footsteps can be heard, the slapping of the soles loud against the terrazzo flooring. We were quiet for a few minutes, my sister pacing behind me. She might just be angrier than me but hides it better.

"I'm sorry."

My eyes snap to his, but before I can answer, Isa's hand moves in my line of sight, and I look over. My sister isn't looking at me, though. Her sole attention is on him. "Are you?"

"More than you will ever understand, Isabella. He was my brother."

"Then why did you give his children your back when we needed you the most?" As she talks, I'm taking in the glossy texture of her eyes, and it has nothing to do with tears. She's here with us, yet she's watching—experiencing what the universe wants her to. That's how her visions work; at any time or place, when they come you have no control. Can't pick or choose. No time to prepare. "And don't tell me you didn't have the chance to reach out. Each of our guards came through here—on the to and from of their journey— and while you gave them housing, not once did you send back word."

"You're hurt, and I accept that, but—"

"You missed his ceremony," I interrupt, gripping my sister's arm to halt her steps forward. "Not that we were able to give him much of one, not with having to run and hide for days on end until reaching the nearest port and taking a ship out of the country. All we could do is pray to Thanatos and ask him to make his journey easy. Not that your brother listens; he still lingers, you know. Waiting. Unable to rest, even after my mother joined him. Her body's resting beside his, but neither was given the rightful burial they deserve from those who love them."

"Doesn't surprise me." Isa's laugh is tinged with sadness. "They've always been needy and unable to rest without our family being complete."

"Will you be there for *that* ceremony? To say goodbye and send them off with peace and love?"

"I don't know yet." But it's not grief I sense in him. It's guilt. *Why?*

"What are you hiding, Uncle? Speak now; please don't force my hand." The tingle starts at the tips of my fingers, traveling up my arm to my shoulder, and then spreads. It's an awakening in my senses, everything becoming clearer, and I no longer see the man in front of me as family.

He's an essence I can manipulate.

And I do. A red haze fills my sight as I stretch out my fingers. The movement calls to his soul, that part of him that keeps him alive.

Because an organ can fail, can be healed by the right person or doctor, but without your spirit, you are nothing.

A shell. Empty.

My uncle's face becomes ashen when I draw out a little of his being, just a smidge, and that small tendril salutes its master with a warm caress of my fingertips. Then more. Enough that he sways, hand clutching at his chest while the word *no* slips past chapped lips.

It would be so easy to end him.

"Please."

"Veritas." One word. A command, and he stumbles back a bit. I'm tempted to force him to his knees, but Isabella opens my hand and intertwines our fingers. My hold on him is still there, but not as choking, and had anyone else touched me, I'd kill them. But not her. Never my siblings. "The truth, Uncle. Why do you feel so much guilt?"

"I've made mistakes I can't take back, Gabriella." He rubs his throat, coughing a bit. "Nothing I will do or say will fix it."

"What things?" Isa speaks from beside me, and I look over. She's a bit more relaxed now, and I'll ask her *why* later. Her reaction before and the still half-gloss effect in her eyes tell me she saw something important. "Who did you hurt?"

That catches my attention, and I flick my eyes back to our uncle. Immediately they narrow at his fidgeting. "Answer her."

"Your father asked me not to get involved. Not until it was time."

"Time for what?" Our uncle opens his mouth to answer but pauses with his sight set on something behind us. For a minute or two, no one speaks, but my patience is thin and I snap my fingers together, causing him to grimace. I still hold a small part of him within my grasp. "Pay attention and answer the question. No more of that vague—"

"Enough of the heavy, my family," Aunt Silla speaks from behind me and I loosen up, yet my glare remains in place. Everything about this conversation is making me suspicious of a man my father loved dearly. "Please come and eat. Let's save the hard conversations until we've all cooled off a bit and you've seen the horses."

"They deserve to know—"

"You have them?" Isa and I say in unison, but it's the surprise in her tone that I focus on. *She didn't see this.* "Since when?"

"Your uncle picked them up a week ago. We'll explain after lunch."

"Now, amore. They need to—"

"I said after, Roberto." She's talking to all of us, yet when I look back, her eyes are on her husband, warning him to defy her request. "We are all hurting right now. We need each other."

He nods, and so do we.

We'll let it rest for now, but I'm not leaving without answers.

Why would my father ask him to abandon us?

Why so much secrecy?

Vampire King
THEODORE ASTOR

"She isn't here, my lord," Brodej says, his foot kicking the back of the knees of this coven's supposed leader. Those same kneecaps hit the ground hard, and his grunts of pain make me smile. "Though the horses out in a small stable wear the royal Wiccan crest. They're meant to appear as such, at least, and yet these are not the ones used by the late king. They're not his."

"Interesting." My eyes survey the scum. His demeanor is proud and he has a false sense of entitlement in his stare, and yet he reeks of fear. He's also young and impertinent, killing his father for the rights to the family home a little over four months ago. A dispute the royal house didn't get involved in, even if the old witch was someone Moore trusted.

That's where his idiocy began. His downfall.

Giving those under your command certain liberties—to feel as though they have a say or are equal—leads to revolt. History always repeats itself.

No group in my kingdom has a leader or voice; I am their God. My word is the law.

The wizard looks away from me, his eyes turning toward the others in the room: his brother-in-law with his wife, his mate holding their small child close, and lastly a woman whose glare is grating on my patience.

Some of these people are innocent. Some are greedy. Reckless.

The latter had been part of Moore's death—engaged in more than one sit-down with a few of the smaller tribes and three others who he fails to name in a documented accord I found inside his desk. The same desk where his father agreed with the fallen king many years ago for a plot of land the older Mariano wanted, before either man had children, in exchange for serving as a high-ranking member of Moore's guard.

I was here for that one as a witness. As an impartial signature.

Something the asshole in front of me isn't aware of.

After every king ascends to power, all others convene. Every race.

An amicable pissing contest to fortify power and amend alliances. We don't have to like each other; I despise all of them...*except* Moore. Him, I could tolerate.

He understood the pecking order, and after such a meeting, I helped with this small matter during that visit.

"Where is she?" At the sound of my voice, the others cower back. Even my men take heed, but none more than the woman and child shaking a few steps from their supposed leader. Their fear is palpable, chokes the room, and he *finally* reacts.

In our world, males are protective over their mates and offspring —an ingrained reaction.

It's why their king came to me. I'm the only one who can protect Gabriella, even if my intentions are morally grey.

"Let them go."

"Tommaso, I won't ask again."

"Vaffanculo." He grits out before spitting at the floor near my feet. His disrespect will cost him. "I'll never tell you."

"Cover her eyes." From my periphery, I see the woman rush to follow my command. Crouching, Tommaso's wife turns the child and hugs her tight, keeping her cherubic face away from us. Then, I'm in front of him before he can react, my hand on his jaw. The bones protest under my grip, grinding a little harder when I squeeze, and I can just make out the subtle crack on the left.

The sound never gets old.

Not enough to hinder his use, but it will hurt throughout our little conversation.

"Let him go, you filthy—" The glaring old bag doesn't get to finish. The female guard standing behind her doesn't think twice and smacks her mouth, the teeth breaking a little—the cut on her lips and gums jagged and very messy. Her screams are garbled, the blood pooling in her mouth before spilling down her chin.

"She smells putrid." My nose scrunches up in disgust. "Her sickness has spread."

"We're doing her a favor." Josephine eyes the woman with nothing but animosity. Her husband, Brodej, does much the same, except his eyes are on the terrified couple. "Once a cunt, always a cunt."

"Personal, Josephine?"

"Not the first time we've met."

I don't ask anything else. Instead, I refocus on the man on his knees before me who tries to speak past my grip. "Something you want to say?"

"Please," he chokes out, body trembling. "My mother—"

Yanking him up by the hold I have on his jaw, I lift him to eye level, feet off the ground. "She's earned the privilege to be here. Would you deny her that right? To be acknowledged for her deeds?"

"Don't hurt her."

"I'm not the one touching her." Before he can speak again, I flip his position so he can face them all. My hand on his neck keeps him in place. His pulse thrums under my fingers. "Yet, her fate is in your hands."

"W-what…" he pauses, swallowing hard "…What do you want from me?"

"You're going to answer a few questions and if you lie, there will be consequences."

"I would never…*fuck*!" Pain-filled screams rend the air a second after I sever his thumb from his hand, the snap of bone from joint loud inside the room while his flesh tears as if it were fabric. One small tug, and it gives under my strength while his body thrashes in my hold, the pain pulsating through every processor.

"Who was involved in the killing of Paolo Moore?"

"If I tell you, I'm dead."

"Wrong answer." Looking over at Josephine, I nod, and she grips the back of Tomasso's mother's head, ripping the white shoulder-length hair half off. From just above the nape of her neck to the crown, the tear is clean, and the missing flesh is now in my guard's hand, a hand that flexes a few times in front of the sobbing, old lady's face. "You're already dead, Mr. Mariano. The torture you receive beforehand, though, is up to you."

"Let them go, and I'll speak."

"Another decision out of your hands." At my words, his wife whimpers, and I look over. Her eyes are on us while she shields her daughter from the sight before her. The woman is brave, her magic is clean, but what surprises me is the anger in her brown eyes directed toward her husband. "I want names."

"Okay."

"And hold your hand up for me while you're at it." He does, but not the bloody one and I correct him with a tap to the cheek. The slap is hard enough to leave a handprint, but I give him credit for just gritting his teeth and taking it like the man he pretends to be. "The other one." Doing as I ask, the thumbless limb rises into my line of sight a few inches from my mouth, and I lick my lips. "Bring it closer."

"Please let them go." My response to that is a snap of my teeth grazing his pointer finger. A few beads pool at the small cut, rolling down, and I breathe in deep. My hunger rises while a growl builds in my chest. *Not yet.* "Your time is almost up."

"The Rossi family." Tomasso's voice is low. A shaky whisper.

"Dead." He looks back at me and gulps. I smirk. "Every guilty party of that clan is dead."

"The Salicios."

"Also dead. No surviving members that I'm aware of, but not by my hand. Seems they had another enemy." Something akin to guilt flashes in his eyes, but it's quickly overpowered by the pain of mourning. "Next name."

Tomasso looks forward again, his eyes glassy. "That's it."

"You're lying." My hold on his neck tightens and I dig a nail into his skin, deep enough that the tip slips inside to the first knuckle while I bring my lips down to his ear. "The truth, asshole. Or I'm going to begin dismembering you piece by piece while your family watches. While your daughter cries out for her father, or will she? They don't seem very fond of you, at least that's what the glare on your wife's face projects."

"I'm telling you the truth," Tomasso manages through my grip. "The blank names never showed up at the meetings. They don't interact with our species."

"And yet they made a pact with you." Eyes closing, he gives me a barely perceptible nod. "This began here with the help of a lover… am I wrong? You and Mrs. Lilibeth Salicio."

"Please stop."

"Lilibeth loved her human mate…" I tsk, sneering at the idiot "…but that didn't stop you from fucking her from time to time and her from easily giving in. Her greed matched your own."

"We were never more than friends."

"So, it wasn't your scent on her skin when I killed her?" I don't miss the way his heartbeat stutters for a moment. The way his body shudders as if in pain at the confirmation that his lover is dead.

A strong hiss comes from someone in the room, and it's not a vampire. No. This is a woman scorned. She's shaking where she now stands, her hold on the girl in her hands wavering for a moment, but his wife's quick to regain composure. "You dirty rotten mother…" the slender woman in a long, green dress takes in a deep breath; she swallows back her ire as the child's quiet whimpers greet the room's ears "…you brought shame and disgrace into our home. You fornicated with a whore, used someone's discontent to your advantage, and then signed our death when you shook hands with those men who hold no—"

"What men?" I ask.

"I don't know them, but one was very powerful. Ancient."

"Shut up!" Tomasso's mother yells then; I scent more than fear on her. It's desperation.

"More than Moore?" I ask, ignoring the old bitch. The wife's low *yes* eliminates a few suspects for me, but it also leaves me with a growing need—a demonic thirst for vengeance that's unsettling. This isn't personal. The attempt wasn't made on me or my kind, and yet it feels as if it were. Nonetheless, I won't stop until I find her. "Cover her ears."

That's all the warning I give as I use my free hand to intertwine my fingers with the fool's and bend his backward. At a steady, painful pace, I force the bones to give—the wrist breaking with ease, and yet I don't stop when his wailing intensifies.

If anything, his weakness is an insult to my very existence.

"Fuck!" There's a resounding crack that makes even Josephine flinch, but I don't pause then either as the bones of his hand are crushed. Each cry from his mouth only serves to further anger me. Each begging plea from his mother's stare makes me prolong the inevitable.

The limb rips, the skin stretching until it can't take it anymore, and then I let go, letting the hand dangle—holding on by a one-inch piece of flesh still connected to the arm. It's a bit grotesque. Very tempting to drink from, and yet, I simply hold it up for his family to watch.

It spurts at first, the red spraying the floor near his mother's foot and she shrinks back, her sobs loud while the others look on with sick expressions.

"I'll talk!" This comes from the couple, and I look over to find the male's eyes on me. He's sweating, face a little pallid at the proof of what I'm capable of, and yet, this is nowhere near my worst. "Please, just let the women go. I'll tell you what I know."

"Were you involved?"

"No, but he told me things."

"Don't you dare!" Once again, it's his mother's threatening words that fill the room.

I've had enough of her.

A quick, sharp whistle rends the air that comes from me, and another entity enters the room. His body slithers along the floor, head held high while everyone else freezes. Even Brodej and his wife aren't completely at ease with the shifter, but they have no say in the matter.

He and his sister have earned my trust.

Are loyal.

The albino python tilts its head, his forked tongue coming out to scent the air.

"What is this...?" the brother-in-law asks, pulling his wife in a little closer. His eyes shifted between the beast and his sister, worried for her and the child's safety.

"The woman and child have ten seconds to leave." At my command, Tomasso's wife exits without looking back at the man bleeding in my hold, while the other woman tries to argue with her husband, but that lasts as long as it takes for my snake to move closer to the pair.

One stretch of its mouth and he pushes her out the room, the move blocking anyone else from leaving. Not that Tomasso or his mother can move. The two are frozen where they're being held, shivering while watching the creature languidly stretch and then lower himself flat to the ground.

Not coiled. Not poised to strike.

He's waiting.

"What's your name?" I ask the brother-in-law.

"Nicolo."

"Well, Nicolo, you've got my attention and I've granted your request. Speak." He swallows hard, his eyes flicking from me to the snake and back again. This also takes longer than it should, something the python gets annoyed by, and in a move Nicolo couldn't predict, it strikes, giving him a warning bite on his leg. Not cutting, but it's enough that the man stumbles back, falling on his ass. "The next one won't be as gentle."

"Tomaso wants the Wiccan crown, believes his family is owed it—"

"Under what claim?" I ask the man bleeding in my hold.

"Before that bastard was born, it was my husband's compensation to take the crown as Moore's right hand! We dedicated our lives, put our goals on hold, and what did we get in exchange?"

"Your husband was never in line for the crown." My hold on her son tightens, and the choking sound—his panic over not being able to get air into his lungs—fills her with renewed rage. "Paolo has a brother and a son, the latter of which is the rightful heir. You have nothing. No claim."

"And all those years served! What about us!"

A low snarl comes from Brodej, and I turn to find his eyes glowing red. His anger and disgust are palpable. "It's a privilege to serve the crown. Any member of the court or guard is proud to do so, and that is what we get—we are honored to keep our people safe and thriving."

She scoffs at that, and I snap the fingers of my unoccupied hand once.

This old woman, a bitter witch, is the reason so many will die. Her greed is why her offspring will witness her last breath a few minutes before following the same fate. They are the epitome of delusional meets blind; she fed him bullshit, and he destroyed them all for a lie with no basis of truth.

Because most lies do hold an element or two of reality, distorted as it may be. The problem here is that even if Moore had no son, his brother would've been the next in line. *Why not his daughters?*

However, there is more to this story.

More people are involved.

"My husband was a fool."

"And you're a greedy cunt." At that, Josephine steps back two seconds before the python strikes, his mouth opening wide and covering her face. Her body thrashes while her son attempts to escape my hold.

Which only hurts him. The last bit of skin holding his detached hand severs and the limb falls, the dull thud barely heard over the scream of utter pain coming from the snake's meal. His body coils around her from just below her shoulders to feet, tighter and tighter, causing the noise to slowly cease, from a high pitch to a low frequency, and then the pressure causes her left eye to rupture.

It pushes out, more with each muscle-tightening move from the snake, and through it all, her son watches on helplessly. His flailing arm splatters my face with blood and my fangs drop, catching a few drops on the very tips.

I lower my lips once again to his ears. "Was it worth it?"

"No." One word. So much pain in his tone. Both physical and emotional. Something I don't quite understand, yet comes in handy. Sentiments have no place in my life; I either trust or end you. No in-between. "Please don't kill her."

Ignoring his request, I release a short whistle and the python tightens his coils. Her face is red, swelling, and the low wheezing of labored breaths follows. Oxygen begins to deplete. Organs are shutting down.

Seconds pass, no more than ten, and her body goes limp. Blood pours from her nose, lips, and eye socket. The back of her skull where Josephine de-scalped her is now a bit coagulated.

Her heart has stopped. Her dark magic is gone.

Nicolo yells her name.

Her son cries for me to stop the predator from eating his meal, a request I consider. "Stop." Everyone stills while I dig my thumb into the wound on Tomasso's neck. He gurgles a bit. "Why should I stop him from swallowing her whole? Why should I let you live?"

"Because I'm not the biggest threat to the twins' lives."

That piques my interest, but not enough to forgive his stupidity. "You're right about that, but you didn't take into account who the bigger predator is. I'm their biggest threat." Walking us closer to his mother's dead body, I pause once we're within reach. "Touch her and say goodbye. This is the last time you ever will."

Tomasso brings his uninjured hand up but pauses at my tsk. "Please, not that."

"Do it."

With a sob, his now torn wrist comes up and he rubs the bloody tip across what's left of his mother's hair. He hisses at the contact, a weird sound between that and pitiful cries. And while he complains, I look over at his brother-in-law who's frozen in place, completely unmoving, and had I not been able to hear his heartbeat, I'd think we scared him to death.

Such a sensitive being.

He will also be useful.

Flicking my eyes back to the snake, I nod, and he releases her mangled face long enough to unlock his jaw. Those milky blue eyes turn darker, lost in his hunger, and bites the top of her head. It works its mouth down, using its razor-sharp teeth to slowly move her down his throat inch by inch.

Moreover, I make the son watch. Up close. Nearly touch them.

"You brought this upon yourselves. Bask in your glory." Tomasso throws up then, his entire body heaving while we take in every moment, from the first swallowed inch until her feet are all that are left. I make sure he doesn't miss a moment before snapping his neck and letting his body fall to the floor.

He's disgusting, dirty, and unappetizing.

Useless to me.

Yet there is someone here I plan to compensate when this is all over.

Looking over at Nicolo, I smile. "Two choices." He nods, tears falling down his pale cheeks. "You can come with me and help decipher the mess your family created. Or, you can choose to be difficult and die."

"My wife…my sister, they'll need—"

"They will be taken care of and untouched, providing you cooperate. You have my word."

Nicolo swallows hard. "I'll go."

"Smart man."

Gabriella

The warmth of a hand settles on my face, its thumb tracing across the apple of my right cheek, and I lean into it with my eyes closed. This touch is familiar to me, and so is the scent of the owner; a delicious essence of earth, spice, and a hint of citrus that tickles my senses and brings a small smile to my face no matter how hard I try to fight it.

"You're late," I say with a hint of chiding, tilting my face in his direction, and yet I don't see him. My eyelids remain as they are, punishing him for leaving me to bear the wilderness alone. "Did you lose your way?"

"I'm never too far behind, Gabriella." The hunger simmering in his velvet tone sends a shiver down my spine, and I feel it as if it were a caress across my sensitive flesh. It heats, pulls from deep within my chest a small kittenish sound. One I've never made before. "You just don't see it that way yet."

"What does that mean?" At my question, he kneels in front of me *underneath a tall willow tree. I'm not familiar with this one, but it calls to my nature, and I couldn't stop the temptation to feel the earth that it grows in. My fingers are embedded into the dirt, the blades of grass tickling my wrist, and yet since he appeared, all I sense is him.*

The cries for attention of those souls needing help cease.

The sorrow and concern of my family disappears.

This stranger gives me peace.

His strong legs stop mere inches from mine, and I open my green eyes to take in the dark pants covering his skin. How thick the muscles of his thighs are, large and strong, and then I trail higher over his narrow waist while ignoring the bulge that gives a harsh jerk under my heated stare. This man is rugged—a heavy sense of power radiates off him while covering me in a blanket of comfort that I won't question.

Who is he?

"You'll know soon enough." It's a purr, a low vibration that moves the very dirt that I now fist. "We will meet, Gabriella."

"When?"

"The signs are already there. Follow them." I try to look up at his answer, but as my stare traverses his six-pack, I'm met with beautiful dark markings that cause me to pause. They tattoo his flesh with intricate feathers that seem to wrap around him from behind, like dark prince's wings, and end just below his ribs. Then, there are the symbols across his pecs and down his sternum that I don't quite understand yet—they're very ancient—but I want to. Can't stop myself from reaching out, fingers dirty with the soft soil of the earth and I rub the one close to his belly button from right to left.

My movement is slow, almost reverent, and I revel in the way he shivers for me.

"Will you tell me about these?" I can't look away from each piece. How the ancient markings create a cohesive design that tells a story, the history of a stranger I need to know. All of him. Every last secret. "Who are you?"

The warmth on my face disappears then, the touch I crave close, but just out of my reach. "You already know."

"How can that be?" I'm leaning toward him, yet when I attempt to look up at his face, the world turns black. My sight is gone, yet he remains. Before I can complain, his breath is on my lips, and instinctively, I lick them. His essence. "What's happening to me?"

"You can't fight fate, Gabriella."

I awake with a start, my heart beating wildly inside my chest while my hands clench tight. The dirt between my fingers suffers my distress, the sudden heaviness in my chest. "What the hell was that?" *Or better yet, who?*

"Gabby?" Isabella calls out not far from me, and my eyes snap up in her direction. Her expression is wary but understanding. "We need to go, sister."

"I need a moment." Voice hoarse, I close my eyes and try to find my center, but it evades me. Instead, anxiety slams into my chest with the vengeance of a beast, stealing the very breath from my lungs. "This dream I had...it's—"

"You saw him?"

"How do you know it's a him?"

"Because I've had a similar dream; the sign I've been waiting for and who I must seek."

"Isa, no more riddles or half-truths. What's happening?"

"That was our mother's dying gift, Gabby. She's pointing us in the direction we must travel and allows us a chance to go there in our dreams. To see what we can't during waking hours."

It dawns on me then and my skin turns ice-cold, a gasp lodging itself in my throat. "King Astor? Why would she send me to a murderer?"

"Because you can't fight fate."

I ignore the pang in my chest at those words, the same ones she's been preaching and the man in my dream crooned. They continue to make an appearance. Mocking me. "He'll imprison me."

"Only you can make him end it all."

"We don't know that—"

"I do." Her expression is resolute. Leaves no room to argue. "Please trust."

"WE'LL SEND WORD IN A WEEK." I give my aunt and uncle pointed looks a few hours after my afternoon nap, my mind doing all it can to push away the memory. The meaning. "Keep him safe. Let me down, and—"

I know my distrust is hurting our aunt—both of them—but they've done a good job of avoiding the conversation my sister and I are owed. Always staying within hearing distance of Leo.

"He'll be safe, my niece. I swear it." Aunt Silla takes one of Isa's hands and one of mine in hers, giving each a squeeze. Her eyes hold the truth. Her scent remains calm, yet I continue to sense the distress in her husband. "No one will come near him, and please trust that we love you three as if you were our own. It's why he brought the horses back; your uncle knew how special they are to—"

"*Why* do you have them?" Isa asks, her tone a bit accusatory yet low enough to not draw attention.

"Vampires have been lurking for a few weeks, just watching, but weren't quick enough this time. A guard saw two in the shadows within the city limits and rushed over, helping us retrieve them—we left behind imposters before they could be taken by King Astor." She looks away from us and toward her husband and our brother. "Please be careful, my nieces. Darkness looms close, and I fear for your safety. You need to head home and bring back peace."

"Peace?"

"You three are the key to our survival."

As the royal family, we are connected to all the witches under our rule, but our senses become heightened with family. I can't hear their thoughts, but their emotions can be felt—smelled as if it were a perfume.

The happier and calmer they are, the sweeter the scent.

If scared or hurt, it becomes a bit bitter or acrid.

"Thank you. Your word is binding." Isa knows my true mood, though, her eyes shifting between me and who I'm staring at. The horses have been wrangled, with two of our guards staying behind. My sister and I will each ride one while the third goes to the man who used to protect our queen. Augusto had been away visiting his mother when our home was ambushed, helping her after a nasty fall, something that eats away at him although he's not at fault. We don't blame him. His loyalty is unwavering, though, and since locating us in England, he's been our shadow. The one guard that never switches to take rest. "Please don't disappoint us."

"We won't." If she's offended by my mistrust, she doesn't say a word. Our pain is still raw—for every member of the Moore family —but at the moment, it's us who've been dealt the harshest of blows.

Our parents. Our home. The feeling of safety.

All gone.

"Much appreciated." Isa stays with her as I walk off after responding, heading toward my uncle and brother who are speaking with Augusto. The latter is showing my brother a small spell all kids learn early on, but for some unknown reason, my brother cannot heal the earth. Not yet, at least. All Wiccans can manipulate nature up to a certain extent, grow plants, and cleanse decay, but his control is as volatile as a baby's.

"One day, I'm going to raise an oak a thousand feet high and strand you at the top," my brother grumbles, his eyes glaring at the two older males who are chuckling. "This is a vow."

"You will, young prince." Augusto nods, head slightly bowed toward Leo.

"Your father was just as stubborn, and look where that got him, nephew. You'll make a fine king one day."

For some reason, those words rub me wrong and my eyes narrow. *Look where that got him?*

However, before I can ask, all three heads turn in my direction. I put a smile on my face and decided to talk to Isa about this later. She's given me her word that Leo will be safest here, and I trust her blindly. "It's time to go."

"Already?" Leo asks, his face falling a bit. I know he's worried, scared we could be hurt, but I ignore the guilt gnawing at my insides. *He's just a kid. He shouldn't be dealing with any of this.* "Can't you stay until tomorrow?"

"We have people to help, little brother. They need us." His expression turns somber at my words but gives me a small smile in understanding. No matter what, those under the ruling of the Wiccan throne come first. "We'll be together soon enough, I promise, but right now I need you to be brave and give me a hug."

Before I'm done talking, he's already crashing into me, almost knocking us both to the ground. "Blood and pact," he whispers low so only I can hear, and I kiss the top of his head.

"We are one. Always."

Leo lets me go then and heads toward Isa, stunning her from the impact while our aunt walks away to give them privacy. And while my siblings talk, I turn to look at my uncle.

"Never find yourself at the end of my wrath."

"Gabby, I loved him."

"Then prove it."

AUGUSTO STOPS his horse just past the entrance of the Salicio territory near our home in Foresta di Ferràina. The place is so quiet, and if it weren't for the royal guards watching the entrance, I'd think the town is deserted. Their heads bow as we pass, swords lowering, but the sheer hurt and anger radiating off their skin is near suffocating.

Something isn't right here. More so than the deceased—the headless bodies drained of all blood that litter the ground. They drank from or let them bleed out from wounds, but the nagging in my gut tells me that there's more to this massacre and I might not be ready to accept it either.

My eyes shift around, taking in the two male warlocks moving their hands in a circular pattern, their lips moving as they sing an incantation. I can just make out the words on their lips, the repeated request that this land is protected and cleansed.

The latter surprises me.

How could this have happened? The scene is out of the norm from the vibrant and happy people whose bloodlines have lived here for over a century, and yet, it doesn't take long to understand why.

Bodies. So many bodies are littering the vast land no matter where we look.

More than the original number given to us in the report.

In front of houses. Tossed against trees. A small pile to the left of where my horse neighs.

A river of dried red dirt shows the path of destruction left behind by the fucking leeches hunting me and my siblings down. How could our people team up with them and do this? This carnage is despicable. Unforgivable.

My heart breaks all over again.

Dismounting my horse, I ignore Augusto's low curse and walk toward a house I'm familiar with. This is the elder's home; he and his wife live here along with two children they adopted who are no older than ten and who've become their sole pride and joy. Their only daughter died a few years ago, nearly killing them.

I studied with her and taught her how to tether a spirit in case I ever needed help.

I trust her and pray that her family is still alive. *They're not. I'm almost certain.*

"Let me go in first, Miss Gabriella." My head turns toward Augusto, and I wave him forward, clutching onto Isa's hand who now stands beside me. We rode straight through without pause, my father's blessed horses going full throttle from Naples toward our beloved lands so we could reach this town. "Please keep behind me, and if we find anyone alive—"

"You will, but not here." A sharp pang hits me straight in the chest at my sister's statement. "I've seen it."

"Of course, Miss Isabella. Do you know where we should start?"

At his question, my sister's eyes close and she inhales deeply and then exhales. Then again. We stay like that for a short while as she centers herself, but when her blue orbs snap open with a glazed-over appearance, I know she's lost in a vision.

They come to her like that. While my father had to touch you, physically be in your presence to see into your life's path, Isabella has the ability to concentrate on what she needs to see. There are also the times when the gift of sight comes at the most random times, slamming into her mind and showing her the inevitable.

"You can't change fate." Her voice is low, and yet I hear her loud and clear. "We can't challenge it either."

Ignoring her warning, I clear my throat. "Sister, what do you see?"

"The center of the village is where we'll find answers." A bit vague, but we follow, careful as to not step on anyone in the path. Two other royal guards fall into step behind us, but it's their low muttering that catches my attention.

"Something you need to say?"

The older of the two steps beside me, his head inclined in my direction. "Princess, we've searched the entire place, house by house, and found nothing." He's not being disrespectful in his doubt, but most only see what's in front of them. If Isa found something, it'll be where she's leading us.

"Do you not trust her? Us?"

"Yes." No doubt or hesitation. Good. "With our lives."

"Then please continue to do so."

"Yes, Princess."

The man retakes his stance a few steps behind me, the guard to his left also quiet now as we traverse the main street toward the center of this village. We ignore the death all around us for now; the bodies can't be moved until I release their souls to the underworld, but the men here today know that a funeral procession must begin immediately after.

The closer we get to our destination, my skin begins to prickle with awareness, though.

I feel life all around me. Not just death.

There's a strong undercurrent that reaches out to me, and my hands clench, eyes scanning the area, but I come up empty. *She's not wrong. Someone is here.*

Isa stops in front of nature's gifts: a beautiful secular olive tree that's grown leaning over, almost at a complete arch. The base is wider than any other in the area, strong, and holds caverns that could fit a person or two inside. *Perfect for hiding.*

"Inside?" I ask, but she doesn't answer. Instead, she walks around while keeping her hand on the trunk, feeling around the reachable crevices. From top to bottom, she inspects every single one while we watch. It takes a while, her half-hazy eyes studying every finger-sized hole until one clicks. *The hell?*

The audible shift is heard by all, but more surprising is the opening of a panel to the right of where she stands. It's within the tree, hard, and the entire structure changes to stone before our eyes, the original sculpture nothing but an illusion.

"Holy fuck," one of the guards whispers just as Isabella steps inside after Augusto. The opening is narrow, enough for one person to walk through at a time, and as I step up to the entrance, I place my hand on the hard stone surrounding it.

It zaps me; the harsh shock has me near stumbling from the force. One guard reaches for me while another does as I did and receives the same electrical gift.

It pulses through me, my insides quaking a bit from the charge, and I study it closer. Whoever put up this enchantment either feared for their safety or was hiding something dangerous. *What the hell is going on here?*

"You still feel it?" I ask the man shaking out his hand, his sword now on the floor near his feet. "It's like a sharp bite."

"Yes, Princess." He grimaces, his eyes searching for something along the bottom edge of the structure. They widen when he does, understanding settling in them. "It's very painful, but magic that old is expected to be."

"What do you mean? Have you seen—"

"Gabby! Come quick!" My sister's scream cuts off any question I have. I'll ask later. There's a lot I still don't know, a sorceress never stops learning, and something about this—the strength behind the ward—is calling to me. The feeling merges with the never-ending pulse that runs through my body—those alive and dead—I sense them all but was taught by my mother to ignore.

To not let myself be swept away by the endless cries or the thrums of heartbeats.

"No one in or out until you see us. Understood?" They both place a hand over their heart in acquiesce, shoulders pulled back as they take their place blocking the door.

"Gabriella, hurry!"

"Coming!" I rush down a second after, making sure to not touch anything. Immediately upon entering, I find a semi-lit staircase leading down, the area just as narrow as the entrance, the steps a little steep, but I follow the path while heading toward my sister's voice. She's speaking to someone. Not angrily, but with concern, and once I reach the bottom landing, I understand why. "Gods above." The sight in front of me is more than heartbreaking. Every cell in my body ignites in fury; the blood in my veins burns me where I stand as the women and small children huddle closer in fear.

There's quite a few of them, all a little dirty and looking hungry but alive and right now, that's what I'll focus on. *Get them out.* The voice in my head makes me pause, my eyes darting around, but I find no one looking directly at me.

It's not Isa either.

"Gabby, we need to leave this place. They need help."

"Whatever needs to be done. No question, sister." A woman whimpers then, and my head snaps to the left but I find nothing. Nothing but a wall and an old oil sconce that's burning bright, although the glass is empty of any flammable material. My feet move toward the door, and I take no more than three steps when a woman rushes out of the group and grips my arm.

Her hold is tight. Eyes look crazed. "If you touch that, we will all die."

Placing my hand over hers, I relax my posture and keep my stare soft. "I'd never allow harm to come to those who are innocent. Please trust me."

"He promised that if anyone touched—"

"Who?"

"Elder Salicio." Thank God her eyes close then as she takes a breath, because every muscle in my body locks and eyes narrow. Not at her, but at that sick bastard who did this. *How long have they been kept like this? How did my father not know?"* "We're kept here to perform for the coven. Our blood protects the grounds."

"What did you just say?" Isa says from beside me then, which I'm thankful for because anything out of my mouth would scare them. Make this much worse for a group of people who've been through enough. "Did he use blood magic?"

"Yes." Her eyes shift nervously toward the others still huddled—shaking—against the back wall. They're watching Augusto, the children crying at their legs, and he's smart enough to stand against the opposite wall and out of the way. "That's how he keeps everyone out of here. No one sees the truth, but his soul is black and his hunger for power is even more dangerous."

"He's dead." The words slip past my lips. I haven't seen the body as of yet, but I know it to be true. That's what I felt earlier when I touched the wall. The magic here is without an owner, a direct source of sustenance, and is volatile. Angry. "You have nothing to fear…?" I trail off, not knowing her name.

"Canalia." A sudden deep sigh escapes her, and the tense shoulders from a few seconds ago drop. "My name is Canalia."

"Nice to meet you, Canalia. We'll discuss the rest of this later as you'll be traveling with us home, but for now, I need you to help me with something."

"My body is weak. I don't have the blood—"

"I'd never ask that of you." The expression on her face is perplexed and my heart constricts; I can't imagine everything these people have been through. "All I need is for you to speak with them and help us get them outside. Can you do that?"

"Yes, Miss Gabriella."

"Thank you, and it's just Gabby. Okay?" At my request, she nods and then turns to speak to those scared and hungry behind her. And while she does that, I look over at Isa, whose expression mirrors my own. Total and undeniable sorrow.

"This is a nightmare." Her cold hand grips mine, a sign she's exhausted. "How could we not know? And are you sure he's dead? Cause I want to—"

"They are all that remains of this clan." Pulling my hand from hers after a minute, I walk over to the sconce and place it on the wall. It burns me, but no mark appears on my flesh and yet the pain is nearly unbearable. It's his doing that I feel this, the turbulent famine of an unfed blood pact, but I hold strong. *Sanguis ad vos reverteur.* The ground shakes, and the screams of those women cause tears to spill from my eyes. I'm returning what belongs to them—their essence and sacrifice will help those victims sustain themselves until we get them home and under medical care. *Sanguis ad vos reverteur.* The light flickers out and my knees shake a bit, but my sister is there with support. Once again, she links our hands, feeding me her energy while her own levels are low. The last few months have left us in a state of exhaustion, and every death and lie surfacing is a hit to our body like the lash of a whip. *Sanguis ad vos reverteur.*

All noises cease then before a low groan meets our ears, and my shaky body takes a step back. The room feels lighter, less repressed, and right when I turn to look at those in the corner, I sense another presence. The place where the old lantern had been is now an open doorway, and I can just make out the shape of someone on the floor.

They are bound; the chain rattles when they move slowly, as if afraid to do so.

"We won't hurt you," Isa says while moving closer, but that scares the person. They whimper and it's a female inside, the sound low and feminine. "No one here will."

"Please let us help you," I add, my tone soft.

"They're here to help, Meera. Don't fight them." Canalia's plea gives me a burst of energy and I rush into the dark room, kneeling in front of a woman no one has seen in years. We thought she'd died. My parents attended her funeral, but we did not, having been far away visiting our English grandparents.

Her eyes meet mine, and I know it to be true. When we were young, she babysat for us.

And all these years…

Bruises and bones—they've reduced her to nothing more than a skeletal version of herself.

"Gabby?" she croaks, voice rough from disuse. "Is that you?"

"It's me, Meera. It's me, and we're getting you all out of here."

Her body shakes, the metal clinking from the movement. "But Dad—"

"He's dead," I hiss out through clenching teeth, my hands extended back, and Isa knew what I needed, placing a blanket in my hand. I cover her. Give her the modesty she's been denied for so long. "And had he not been, I'd be running a sharp blade across his neck."

"Thank you."

"Don't. I'm sorry it took us so long to find all of you." Augusto enters the space then, and she stiffens, so scared. He stills, giving her time to calm down while looking at me for permission to carry on.

Her anxiety is palpable, near choking, and I tip her face in my direction. "He's just here to get you out of those chains. Please let him help you."

"Okay."

"Focus on me, Meera. I won't fail you again."

Gabriella

The second we enter our lands after twenty-four hours of rough travel back home, the women and children too fragile to walk for long periods, Isa and I head straight for the throne room. The guards have their instructions, and word has been sent back to those on our lands of the women and children coming back with us. And while these—our people—need words of comfort and support, our grief is too strong to contain.

It's been months since we were driven from our home in the dead of night.

It's been months since they killed the two people we needed most in this world.

Death and ash still suffocate the home where we grew up, and although it's been cleaned and emptied of damaged items, nothing can erase what I feel. What my sister still sees.

Their beautiful, ornate high-back thrones are gone.

The windows, the stained-glass panes with the depiction of my mother's favorite olive tree, are blown out and the wooden frame completely charred.

All lighting is broken and the floors cracked.

No one speaks as we walk toward the center of the home. Even the young, who have slowly grown comfortable within our group, are now quiet and somber. Their eyes follow us, their hearts holding the same pain, but it's not until one by one they follow our path that my tears begin to fall.

They form a circle around our bodies in the center of the large room and begin to chant. Their affirmation—affection—for us is touching, and I find solace in it. So does Isabella, drying her eyes before falling back into line with the circle, her body swaying a bit as she joins them.

Ut anima tua inveniat pacem. May your soul find peace.

And I hope we do. That it rains down upon our people and brings back the prosperity and security stolen by the greed of others.

The low voices merge, the cadence so beautiful, and my heart weeps for a different reason.

We aren't alone.

We will rise from this tragedy and avenge our loved ones.

I vow this silently while joining hands with Canalia and a little boy no older than eight who bears a strong resemblance to her. They both grip my fingers tight, giving me the strength I need as my heart weeps for every person with us and those lost to senseless violence. Greed.

Slowly, my voice nothing but a whisper past the lump in my throat, I join them. From one conjuration to the next, we fall seamlessly into the words needed to protect our land and those who reside here. Our barriers are weak. Our faith is shaken.

You can't fight fate.

Our voices rise as if following the heavy thrum of an invisible drum, slow to volatile, and only calming the raging waters once an invisible snap runs through our chain. It's a sharp shock, grappling with our equilibrium, but our coven remains, giving strength to those younger and older who need it.

We remain quiet for a few minutes, each person breathing deeply in and out, clearing our lungs and welcoming the lighter feeling inside the home's walls, this sense of security that protection brings. Just like the last time Dad renewed it after our grandfather passed away.

With death comes a time of cleansing.

They need to rest. The family needs to find solace.

A low sigh across from me pulls me back to the present, and I meet my sister's stare head-on. There's resolve and a touch of sadness in her blue orbs with the knowledge of what the future holds.

You can't fight fate.

"It's time." Her words, although expected, still land like a punch to the gut.

"Can we have tonight?"

"That's all we'll have." Those around us watch but don't ask questions, yet the curiosity is there in their unwavering stare. "Tonight we will visit with you, but tomorrow we must leave."

"But where will you go?" Canalia is the first to speak up, the others slowly doing the same.

However, it's Meera who's the loudest. Those eyes have seen so much, things I couldn't even begin to imagine while being her father's captive and main blood donor, but in them, I find understanding and respect.

Her small hand goes up, and the others cease all noises. "You've seen the answer, Isabella." Not a question. A statement for those inside the room. "Will this save us? Will all the deaths end and those guilty be brought to justice?"

"Yes."

"Then do as you must." Meera moves toward us, those around her watching her every move. Worried she'll fall, and it warms my heart to see them ready to step in when they are just as hurt or in need of help. "We're here for you the way your family has always stood for us. No king shall break that."

Those words help me find the strength—the resolve to leave and seek he who wishes to own me. If she can stand tall after everything, after the horror-filled way we found her, then I can face him.

I will find a way to end this nightmare.

"Everything will be back in its rightful place after this trip. The truth will set us free." Isabella's emphasis on the word *truth* isn't lost on me. Yet the quick flick of her eyes toward me tells me it isn't the right time to ask.

We'll talk.

Later.

When these people are fed and resting. After visiting our parents' resting place.

"And we will stand in your absence. We will protect your home and honor your parents until you return."

A SMALL TAP to the Salernitano horse I'm riding brings him to a halt near the forest edge of the vampiric kingdom's castle. He neighs a bit, almost as if pleading me to turn and go, but I scratch between his ears instead as I appraise the area. It's quiet. Almost eerily so, but they won't sense me while I wear my mother's opal stone with a concealing spell.

You can see me, but not sense—smell—me.

Another braying sound, this time accompanied by a stomp of his foot. Onyx is unsettled, his attention flicking beyond the trees, and his unease means someone is close. Too close.

"Videam," I whisper, my eyes trained on an area not far from where I'm hidden behind a large tree. The greenery here is overgrown, the vegetation thick and dense.

It takes a minute or three, but soon enough a guard walks past without pausing. He's in a dark red—almost black—uniform with a large sword strapped across his chest, but that's not what captures my attention. No. What I'm captivated by is this hint of cedar and citrus that infiltrates my senses.

It's familiar, yet I can't quite place from where.

He walks with purpose; eyes ahead and back straight, not once turning in our direction before disappearing through another thick cluster of bushes. *It could be a trap.* He's heading in the direction away from the coast and the large palace; I blink, and it's as if he'd never been there.

No noise. No one else passes through, and after a few minutes, I dismount the horse. "I'll be back, Onyx. Behave." His answer is akin to a snort, and I scratch down his nose, my touch soft. "No backtalk. This is an in-and-out operation, and I need you to be alert."

At least, that's my hope.

Giving him one last gentle pat, I turn and walk in the opposite direction of the man. The closer to the large castle I get, the temperature seems to drop, the waters off the coast creating a cooling mist.

Within minutes I'm at the border and in open space, my eyes shifting from left to right, taking account of the stillness of the night. To be honest, I thought it'd be busier.

Vampires are known to hunt at night. Embrace the demon behind the facade of a regal disposition.

"No matter what, Gabby, you need to reach King Astor," Isabella says, sitting in the family mausoleum on the property. No one is allowed inside aside of blood ties, and there are only three of us left. We've been here awhile now with a few candles lit, the souls of our parents close by and flicking through each fiery wick. The fire dances —rises—with their agreement and blessing. "He will listen. He's the key."

"How can that be, when so many lives have been lost because of him?" I hiss out, my anger creating havoc with the spirits lingering near us. However, the loss of our people isn't something I can get past—it tears my soul apart. There's a sudden burst of wind near me that makes me pause, though, as the room grows colder. "I'm okay."

She sits forward, her expression understanding. "Control your-self, sister. Not everything is as it seems."

I bite back a scoff. This isn't her fault. "So we imagined the complete massacre at the Salicio village?"

"Did you forget that Meera's father was dealing in blood magic? That he sacrificed the women and children to—"

"I haven't." Voice low, I meet her eyes through watery ones. The sight, the smell inside that hidden prison will forever haunt me. "Had we found them while Salicio himself was alive, I would've done worse."

"Then don't judge." Isabella sits back again. Her posture is a little less rigid. "Justice was served."

"And the others?" I breathe in deep to rein myself in. "That man is a monster."

"Do you trust me?" she counters, and I nod, even though every fiber of my being rejects the notion of pleading—allying with this man. No good could come of this. "Then stop fighting fate."

My parents return to calmness at that, their essence once again resting.

"Okay." It's done. Decided. "And you? Where are you—"

"I have a werewolf to tame and a pack to win over."

Vampire. Werewolf.

"This is insanity," I mutter under my breath, my footsteps light as I walk through the open back door. The opulence is apparent the moment you step inside; all golds and black wallpaper with a touch of red on an accent wall that I find disturbing. *Is it blood or paint?*

A shudder runs through me at the thought, yet I don't pause, and continue walking down a long hallway that leads to a grand foyer. A staircase is at the center, the paths separating at a landing a few feet up and then going right or left. The banister is tall and imposing, all in a black wooden tone that's two tones lighter than the walls with a gargoyle's head as an ornamental detail atop each of the larger balusters.

Step by step, I head on up and then go right. Don't know why, but I do and the silence, the lack of occupants, begins to unnerve me.

Either this is a trap, or he's too confident.

Moreover, I'm wondering what poor kingdom is feeling the wrath of his search. He's been looking for me incessantly, plowing through small covens in search of me, although we're hiding in plain sight.

Not once has he stepped foot inside Moore's land. Why? That alone lets me know that he's trying to catch me off guard. That if caught, I'd be taken against my will, and I won't let others suffer for his greed. *This ends today.* Fate led me here, but I'll decide the outcome.

No one else will die.

"Pompous, arrogant jerk," I grumble, stealthily walking the hall toward the vampire king's bedroom. This floor is large with only one door and the essence lingering throughout is domineering and intimidating. Powerful. *This has to be his.* "Like I don't have better things to do than come and kick his butt."

His room is closed when I reach it and I don't hesitate to step inside, closing the large wooden door behind me. The first thing I notice is his scent; it permeates the room and calms my nerves at once—the woodsy aroma with citrus is stronger here and reminds me of the guard outside.

Is that how all vampires smell? How they lure you in? I frown at the thought. It doesn't sit well with me.

Dad kept us away from them for a reason, and this might be it.

I can't deny that it's tempting my senses.

Another deep inhale, and a small keening sound leaves the back of my throat. This isn't what I expected, how the masculine fragrance settles at the core of me, and I find myself *liking* it.

I can't control it. My eyes close of their own accord for a second, just enough to clear the sudden fog, which I shake off before reopening them again. This time, I focus on the size of the room and its bland décor.

Not a single trace of femininity anywhere.

"What makes you tick, Theodore Astor?" I ask myself, taking a seat on his bed as if it's the most natural thing, nearly sinking into the plush bedding. "What would it take for you to—"

The bedroom door slams open then, cutting me off as a large man steps inside, his warning snarl loud. The walls shake, and I let out a whimper. Not in fear, but for some reason, it makes my skin prickle with excitement. *What the hell?*

"Who are you?" he asks, his voice low and tone a bit gravelly. It licks at my skin, an illicit caress while the blade of his sword glints in the low light. "Why are you in my bedroom?"

"You've been looking for me, Theodore," I state simply, my hand slowly moving toward the small holster at my side where my knife hides. "So here I am."

"Have I?" he asks, not fully stepping into the light. He's in shadow, but those amber eyes glow and his strong build is mouthwatering. "What's your name, pretty girl?"

"Come a little closer and I'll tell you." There's no mistaking my breathy tone nor the way I cross my legs, the skirt of my dress parting at the split to reveal the side of my thigh and lower. Moreover, he follows the move with hunger, his chest expanding as he takes in a deep breath. "This conversation needs to be face to face."

In a flash, he's kneeling at my feet, his hands on the bed trapping me while my knife is at his throat. If he's surprised, he doesn't show it, nor does he try to disarm me. "Can you tell me now, my queen? I need to know my mate's name."

"Mate?" I ask, the blade digging a little deeper, an action that hurts me. *He can't be right. How?* "You're mine?"

Is that why my heart is beating fast?

Is this why my palms are sweaty?

Is this why I find his dark, black hair and amber eyes so sexy, and the thought of hurting him makes me feel sick?

I'm going to kill Isabella for hiding this—for letting me think he'd be agreeable to an alliance. Because I am certain she knew. Had to.

Mates are a special thing, a gift, and there's no denying the need you feel. It's all-consuming and sudden and unforgiving as you give yourself without pause or consequence. A few words and your world changes, an instant love that gives your life true meaning.

"I'm yours." His smile is beautiful and the look in his eyes so soft, a complete contradiction to the man who's been pillaging in his search for me, threatening covens under my family's protection, and terrorizing them into telling him where I am while failing at every turn.

They're loyal to us. They'd never sell me.

They died to protect us.

Didn't they?

The Salicios, Marianos, and Rossis all turned out to be enemies.

But how can he—this vampire—be my mate? How do I forgive and move past everything?

Gods, I'm confused.

"And again, you've been looking for me. Why?" At my words, spoken low and a bit sultry, his eyes snap from my lips to my eyes, widening as they sink in.

"Gabriella?"

"Theodore."

The minutes pass and neither of us speak, too lost in our thoughts. However, it's his hand on my cheek that calms me just when I think it's better that I run. It's the feel of his lips on my neck and the arms around my waist that anchor me as the knife slips from my fingertips, clanging on the floor.

So simple each touch, but from your mate—the one person made for you—it gives your soul purpose.

"I'm sorry." He says it so low I almost don't hear it, but I do, and a shuddering breath escapes me. This is the last thing I expect from the proud king, but right now he's humbling himself while the sword he held moments ago is now astride my lap. An offering. "You are the lesson I needed to learn, Gabriella Moore. My life is yours."

"Theo, I—"

"Say it again." His purr-like rumble tickles, creates a vibration through me that makes me laugh. "Please."

"Since when does a king beg?" I ask, and this flirtatious side of me is new. *This is inappropriate. So wrong.* And so is the way I clench at the sight of his harsh swallow—the delicious way his throat bobs with the action.

I need to reject the—

He pulls back so I can meet his eyes. I see the sincerity in them, and it nearly bowls me over. "Since the moment I laid eyes on you."

A blush spreads across my cheeks, and I bite my bottom lip. "Does this mean you'll stop hurting innocent people?" *Please don't disappoint me.*

"This means my life is yours to command, pretty girl."

"That's a hard offer to deny, Mr. Astor…"

"Then don't." He lifts me with ease, tucking me against his chest while seating me on his lap. We're on the floor, his body cradling mine while those lips kiss from the crown of my head to the temple. "Let me love you. Let me be the one you lean on."

"You've hurt my people."

"And I will make the reparations necessary to those who are innocent." With the tip of two fingers, he nudges my head so we're eye to eye. His lips hover, and I can taste him there. His natural sweetness is a tease to my senses. "Let me spend an eternity making you happy."

"What will it cost me?"

"Your heart, and in return, I'll give you all of me."

Vampire King

THEODORE ASTOR

Fuck, she's beautiful.

My eyes take in every stunning inch and for the first time in my life, I'm thankful to the man who fathered me. Because without his selfishness, I would've never been given such a treasure.

My life is no longer mine.

She's curvy, I can tell even from my kneeling position at her feet and the high slits of her dress that end just below the edge of each hip. It's provocative, this thin garment with a plunging neckline and access to her body—a temptation I'm finding hard to resist.

Every time she inhales, my resolve breaks a little more.

Every time she blinks, I find myself wrapped by an enchantment I can't fight.

Moreover, the words I've said in the past about mates are all bitter pills to swallow.

My eyes travel from her fiery red strands to the expressive green eyes looking at me with heat and then lower, to her small button nose. I count the small smattering of freckles across the bridge there before taking in the plumpness of her soft-looking lips and the straight line of teeth embedded in the sweet flesh.

My mouth waters and my chest expands again, pulling that sweet scent of cherries with sweet vanilla cream into my dead lungs like an addict. Because I am one. My purr of satisfaction is proof enough.

A both humbling and lascivious sound.

Her scent is as appetizing as her blood.

Both sing to me. They demand that I move a little closer, and I do, my body slowly pushing hers back on the bed as I crawl over the supple curves I will worship for eternity.

Mine. She's all motherfucking mine.

My fangs descend and that content purr turns into a hungry hiss, a warning to the world of my intentions. This pretty girl has no idea that she's just become the apex predator; she controls me.

"Theodore." It's a sigh. So sweet. I shudder above her, my hands immediately finding purchase atop the bed at each side of her head. I'm her personal cage: a prison she'll never escape. "You feel so good. Just feeling your skin close to mine is heaven."

"That's because I was created to one day worship you." Her thighs open and my hips punch forward; she's cradling me, and her heat causes my eyes to roll back. "To bring you pleasure."

I'm right there. Her softness sears me.

Looking down, I take in the way her dress exposes her. Her skin is on display, the supple curve of her thighs teasing me with the subtle clenching of the muscle there. Then, there's the hint of wetness coating her thighs, the heightened sweetness causing a deep, animalistic rumble to form in my chest. The sound makes her shiver, makes her upper body arch up and the pointed tip of her breast to rub against mine.

"Motherfuck," I growl at the feel of her. The hand to the right of her head moves down to her hip and grips it, my hold tight—a bit painful—but the way she moans low is proof she likes it. That my beautiful doll isn't breakable. Christ, I shake above her—my entire body pressing deeper into her, and I feel it, the lack of undergarments.

She's bare beneath the thin material. A dress that's tight, the long skirt molding to every inch of her while those forsaken slits at the sides destroy my senses.

Her mere essence alone breaks my free will.

I never knew—believed—how strong the bond one has with a mate could be.

I'm no longer living for myself, but for her.

Always her. Only her.

"Please."

One word. It destroys me.

From the very tip of her dainty toes to the fiery locks on top of her head, she's perfection.

My mate. Gabriella Moore.

You'll know soon enough that fate is unavoidable. She will surprise you.

"He knew." It's a whisper that causes her brows to furrow, but before she can ask questions, I'm slanting my lips over hers. I'm taking her exhale into my lungs and groaning as the first pure taste of my pretty girl embeds itself into my DNA.

There's a kittenish sound from the back of her throat, and her fingers find purchase on my back, her nails gripping my shirt and pulling me closer. I let her, lowering my full weight, which she welcomes by wrapping those sinful legs around my hips.

They tighten while her lips part and then she's exhaling against me. Her breath is sweet. Pleasure rips through my chest at that, through every fucking limb, and I run my fangs across her bottom lip, creating the smallest cut.

A drop of blood pools on the pink flesh, calling my name, and I don't hesitate to taste. One swipe of my tongue and she quivers, eyes rolling back before I dive in for more. Her taste is an explosion across all my senses; I've never been more of a beast than in that moment, and I take without pause.

It's hard, fucking goes against my every instinct, but I retract my fangs and kiss her with every bit of the passion she ignites in me. The bond sizzles between us and every touch is a spark of electricity that runs through my dead heart, creating a low frequency through my veins. Her tongue meets mine shyly at first, just a small swipe that shows her inexperience, but that one touch renders me her slave.

I'm addicted. Want more.

The hand at her hip traverses up the side of her body, from ribcage to her perky tits, and I swipe my thumb across one. The plump flesh is soft yet firm, and the way she cries out at the simple touch is heady.

It further proves just how untouched she is.

Pure. My little virgin.

I can scent her innocence.

Another soft pass, and then I bring my hand under her back and up until I'm gripping the base of her neck, fisting the soft waves there and forcing her head back. I love this angle. Gabriella's neck is arched, back exposed, and her pouty lips quiver in anticipation.

"Say you're mine," I all but snarl against her mouth, and the pupils of her eyes widen. The scent of want and lust permeates around us. Hers and mine. "Vow it."

"Theo, I—"

"Fuck, pretty girl. Again." The way the shortened version of my name rolls off her tongue is an aphrodisiac. It's hell keeping myself under control; the things I want to do to her, with her, are blasphemous. "Say it."

"Theo, I'm yours and you are mine." No doubt. She says this so prettily.

"We are one." This time it's her who attacks, giving in to her nature while fighting my hold on her head to meet my lips in a feral kiss. It's a sign of her own possession, hunger, and I return the sentiment while acclimating her to my touch. No more gentle caresses, now it's raw and passionate. Our tongues intertwine and stroke, memorize each other—learning—and each pleasurable sigh from her is tattooed onto my flesh, settling on the tip of my hard cock that flexes against her heat.

The bottom of her thin dress shifts a bit, allowing me to press a little harder against her core. She's wet for me, and it seeps through the linen of my trousers, kissing my cock. It flexes and she pulses, our mouths moving in tandem with each thrust.

It feels so good to hold her like this. Even with clothes separating our flesh, nothing has ever felt so satisfying. Frustrating, yet pleasurable.

I want nothing to separate us. To feast on both her blood and pussy, but my beauty is untouched, and our first time will not be rushed. I'd never forgive myself if she regretted having me as her destined.

To the world, I'm a monster, but for her, I'll be gentle. Be the man she needs.

Her hips buck beneath me and her thighs shake. "I'm…This is different than when I—"

"Let go, pretty girl. I have you."

"Help me." Gabriella's sinful plea forces my fangs to drop. I can't stop it. Nature overrides my desire to be gentle and I gift her a harsh nip to the corner of her top lip, raking my sharp tooth over the abused flesh as I thrust again, three times in quick succession.

The skin breaks. Blood rises to the small wound.

"Come for me," I demand before tasting the forbidden fruit once again. Her scream rends the air, her pussy pulsing against my covered length, and it's that sweet sound of rapture that slams into me.

My orgasm is hard and cruel, nearly painful with the need to have her skin on skin, but I ignore it and focus on the way her scent magnifies, infiltrates every nook of my bedroom and settles into the walls. Then, there are the low moans she emits. How she shakes and her fingers pull me closer, her mouth now hovering over mine.

"You're mine," she whimpers. "Only mine."

"Yes." Slowly, I bring her down from her peak. My body

cocoons hers while my lips trail from the edge of her hairline down to her chin. It takes a while for the aftershocks to subside and her body to succumb to exhaustion, but I revel in the moment she does.

Eyes closed, Gabriella looks like a delicate doll, but I now know better. She traveled far to find me, not knowing who I am to her. She's brave and protective of her people, going as far as to pull a knife on me.

My little warrior. My cunning queen.

"I'm going to burn the world to the ground in your name, Gabriella. Gods help those who wronged you because I'm going to enjoy bathing us in their blood."

Gabriella

The sun warms my skin, relaxing me as I sit in an open field full of sunflowers. They sway in the breeze, giving me their sweet scent as two figures walk toward me. I'm not alarmed by their presence. If anything, I'm smiling. A feeling of pure joy reverberates throughout my body.

I missed them.

"You came."

"We are always near, my sweet child," Dad chides softly, his tone indulgent, but there's also a small hint of reprimand there. He holds a hand out for me to take and I do, letting him pull me up and into a strong hug. And at that moment, I breathe for the first time in months without the ever-present sense of choking that's accompanied me since their deaths. "No more crying, Gabriella. We are okay."

"They took you from us." My tears soak his robe, and I'm shaking as grief slams into me with a vengeance, ripping open the wounds I've fought to close. "I can't forgive him. Any of them."

"Punish those responsible, Daughter. Show them who you are."

"Then I must reject him."

Dad gently pushes me back, his hands gripping my arms while my mother steps into my line of sight beside him. "No. You can't."

"But—"

"He is not at fault for our death, Gabby," Mom says, her tone just as gentle and sweet as always. But behind her soft demeanor, there's a warrior. A just and fair Wiccan queen with unfathomable knowledge who's angry at me for some reason. "You're stuck in the past while evading a prosperous future. Open your eyes, love. Open them and see the truth, and not what your pain dictates."

"He attacked the Rossi, Mariano, and Sali—"

Dad scoffs, his hands dropping from my arms and up to my face, caging it in his warm palms. "He did as I asked and killed those who conspired against me."

"What are you talking about?" My brows furrow and I take a step back, then another. I need space. I'm confused. "What did you do?"

"He honored the request of a dying man. The three families rose against us for greed, and King Astor saved you and your siblings."

"Dad, you have to be mistaken—"

"Hush, child. Listen, and open those beautiful green eyes." Mom steps in beside me, hugging me from the side, something she's done a million times in the past. "We knew what the fates had in store for us and accepted, but not without backup plans. He is your other half. Your soul."

"You approve." And I also can't stop the small grin that forms at the realization. Have I truly been wrong all along? *"Why not tell us? Why the secrets?"*

"Because I'd never forfeit my child's life to save my own."

"But I could've—"

"Wake up, Gabriella." Mom nudges my side, and I turn my face to hers. She's glowing. Her smile is blinding. "No more doubts or recriminations. It's time to stop living in the past and embrace him."

"And our people?"

"They will rise once again because of our children. You have always been our biggest blessing."

"Wake up, pretty girl." A pair of soft lips whisper next to my ear, kissing the shell between each word. My eyes open without fuss or complaint, my usual morning crankiness forgotten as the conversation with my parents flows through me.

It's a soothing balm. The weariness—the heartache I've carried for months—is calmer and I once again have peace. And while a part of me will always mourn the lives lost, I no longer blame him.

If anything, I'm ashamed of how quickly I put the fault on him. Owe him an apology.

"I'm up." Voice hoarse, I snuggle back into his embrace while gripping the hand around my waist and bringing it to my lips. I kiss each knuckle. "Thank you for letting me rest."

"Never thank me for taking care of what is mine. Your need always come first."

A small smile forms on my lips, a sassy response on the tip of my tongue. "That's a big statement."

"It's my truth."

Looking back at him from over my shoulder, I arch a brow. *Everyone has a limit, even kings.* "What if I asked you to harm—"

"I'd kill every member of my kingdom if it made you smile."

"You didn't even pause."

"No. I didn't." Even though I'm not a violent person by nature, I'm touched by his willingness to keep me happy no matter the cost. It's sweet in a macabre way. And I'd also like to think he knows I'll never ask for such a thing. I'm just, not cruel. "You'll learn that about me, love. I'm a beast of his convictions."

I don't say anything after that, but the bond between us vibrates with the feeling of contentment; a low vibration that mimics his purr and to which I get lost. There's comfort in it. In us.

The sky outside his windows goes from pre-dawn to the sun blazing high in the sky, and with it comes my rumbling stomach.

The sound is loud in the quiet space, and I blush, knowing he heard.

"I've already ordered your meal, sweetheart. I'll be picking it up soon." There's humor in his velvet voice, and I peek back at him. He's staring at me, the softest look on his face, and it's a complete contradiction of the man I know he is.

I turn in his arms then to get a better look at him. To study every inch of his face; from his dark hair to amber eyes that flick to red and back the longer I stare. They're beautiful, an enchanting ruby that pulls me in and I fall, without doubt or reason. I find myself giving in.

He's mine. Truly made for me.

My eyes shift down a bit, and I take in his lips: pouty and soft, yet the teeth he hides beneath are sharp. A shiver runs through me at the reminder of his fangs, but not in fear or disgust. If anything, I'm wet. Swollen once more for my mate.

I feel the ghost of them sweeping across my lips once again. The way they pricked the skin, the sharp and quick sting, and then the glory of his tongue soothing the nick.

I want them again.

"Do it." The red of his eyes darkens and his tongue wets his bottom lip. "They won't disturb us; the guards and staff know better than to come near this floor until I've had my fill of you and even then, I want you all to myself. I don't share."

I don't share.

Those words cause me to whimper, and I kiss him, my lips molding to his and sucking the bottom one between my teeth. Something in me pushes me to bite him. To sink my teeth in deep even though I don't think he'll feel it as I do, and yet his response is glorious.

Every muscle in his body locks—tightens—and an animalistic growl builds in his chest.

That sound is heady. It causes me to respond with a noise of my own, this kittenish whimper that he soothes by running his hands up and down my sides, pausing on the outside of my breasts as he did a few hours ago, but instead of skimming them, Theo cups each and gives a small squeeze.

Not hard, but just shy of a little pain, and wetness seeps from my clenching hole. It coats my inner thighs and his nose flares, muscles tight, but then I'm pulling back as something registers.

His words.

And while every part of me protests this, my mind won't let up. "Is that why I was able to get in so easily? Because no one stopped me, and I expect more from the vampire king than low protection of his home."

"You seem more at ease." That's his response, no reproach for stopping, and before I can ask him again, Theo shakes his head. He also bops me on the nose affectionately and I pout, already needing another kiss. *Why couldn't I wait to ask?* "Our home is always being guarded, Gabriella. I have eyes everywhere, and yet, you got through without anyone being the wiser. My guess is you either cloaked yourself, which points out a flaw I'm not proud of, or the men on rotation last night dropped the ball and need to be dealt with accordingly. Which one is it, sweet girl?"

"A little of both." I give him a sheepish look, and the man does not react as I expect. Theodore throws his head back on the pillow and laughs, the heavy vibrations rumbling through me, and I can't help but giggle. It feels as though he's tickling me, hitting every one of my weak points and exploiting them to his gain. "Please stop."

His laughter turns into a hum, smirk deepening. "That whine of yours is quite adorable."

"And you're not being fair."

"Maybe that's because you're irresistible and deserve to be punished."

"Punished?" I squeak, and yet the thought isn't unpleasant. I'm a virgin, not a monk, and I've heard enough mated women speak of sex to understand that with the right partner, it's a divine experience. There's also no doubt in my mind after the way he made me come earlier—stole my first kiss—that he's a giver. He enjoyed watching my every reaction to his touch.

"Intrigued?" Once again, my face heats up, but when I try to look away, Theo tsks. With the tips of two fingers, he turns me back, expression serious—a bit of his beast shining through the bright red eyes. *So, bright red for aroused, and the darker tone for anger.* Noted. "Never hide from me, pretty girl. I always want to have those gorgeous green eyes on me. Understood?" I nod, and he makes a low hissing sound of displeasure. "Use your words."

"Yes. I understand."

"Good girl."

"You suck." I'm looking at him from beneath my long lashes, lips twitching, but I keep back my smile. The man isn't playing fair, and I can't deny the way those words affect me. Damn it all, I find the hidden threat a little sexy.

Or maybe a lot. Very much so.

"I will. Promise to bite a little deeper next time, too." No shame. Not lying either.

At once, I flush from head to toe and before I can protest, I'm on my back with a god-like creature above. Looking at me with tenderness, yet behind the softness, there's more.

Heat.

Want.

Hunger.

"You're going to be the best kind of trouble, Miss Moore. The reward I don't deserve but will never forfeit." Lowering his face to mine, he nips my jaw. "But it's time to feed you. I'll be right back."

Then he's gone. Before I can blink the room is empty and the door is closed.

I'm left to my thoughts and how easy things are between us. Feel.

I'm also giddy. Happy.

"Sit up and back on the pillow, please."

"Gods," I scream, having not paid attention, much less thinking that he'd be back so soon. But there he is at the foot of the bed now with a domed plate in his hands, brow arched. "Do I need to put a bell on you?"

"Lost in thought?"

"No."

"Liar." Placing the food atop the bed, he walks over and moves me with ease, propping me against the headboard with a few pillows behind my back. Once he's satisfied I'm comfortable, he retakes the plate and sits beside me, his body turned toward me.

I'm watching him with curiosity, not understanding until the top is removed, and he picks up a bite of strawberry with the tip of his fingers, bringing it to my lips. He rubs it there, a soft caress before pushing it between my lips.

Not that I fight it, my mouth opening for him without hesitation and I chew, licking the bit of residue off his digit before swallowing the juicy bite. And he enjoys it, groaning while offering me the next bite. This time, it's a blackberry. It's sweet with just the right amount of tartness that he adds a kiss to after I swallow.

Each piece of fruit that follows is the same; he feeds me until there's nothing left in the bowl before offering me a buttery croissant with jam a morsel at a time.

He takes pride in this. In caring for me.

Theodore is the antithesis of everything I'd thought he'd be.

Gabriella

"How in control of your gift are you?" he asks me late into the night. The sun rose and set, leaving behind total darkness inside the large room where we lie in bed—something he remedied by lighting a few candles before returning to his preferred place: my chest to his, and his cock nestled between us.

Even through the layers of clothing that separate us, I feel every inch—each jerk—and it's getting harder and harder to not reach out and touch it. The bond pulses, it pulls us closer, and I welcome the sensation—has fast become second nature.

My clothes feel constricting, although my dress is thin and considered seductive by modern society. To my people, though, this is our normal. We don't like restrictions, nor do we push away our nature: the need to feel free and unencumbered by heavy layers that are meant to keep you pure and modest.

Purity comes from within. Modesty comes from self-respect, not thick cotton.

Theo hums to himself then, his fingers trailing down my spine. It feels as though he's counting—memorizing every bump of my spine. "You haven't answered, pretty girl." His voice is low, and his leg is thrown over my hip, our bodies in constant contact while a low purr vibrates through his chest.

The sound is lulling, so calming that I almost ignore the nickname once again. *Pretty girl.*

Just like the warmth that seeps from his skin to mine, he feels good. Like my home—something I'd lost after my parents' death. It's comfort and love and a feeling of internal peace that calms every raging thought or endless worry over what's to come.

I have him. I'm not alone. *Did Isabella have the same luck? Is she okay?*

Lifting my head slightly from its position on his shirt-covered chest, I meet his amber eyes. "Why do you call me 'pretty girl'?"

"Because that's what you are." Lowering his head, he pecks my lips twice. "Do you not like it?"

"I do."

"Do you know why that is?"

I'm shaking my head minutely before he's done with the question. "There's no exact reason, Theo. But I can't deny that my soul sings each time you do."

"That's because you're mine, Gabriella." The smile on his face is beautiful. He's otherworldly. *He's mine.* "The second my eyes met yours, my life truly began. This pretty little thing that I want to circle around and protect—cherish and fuck. I want to devour you, sweetheart. Own you. And yet, above all that, I want to spoil you."

Heat spreads across the apples of my cheeks. I feel it, but I'm not going to deny us. Him. "I want that too. Only with you."

"Good girl." My answer earns me another soft kiss, but this one ends with his sharp, quick nip. "Now, I'm going to need you to answer my previous question. How in control are you of your gift?"

"Very much so..." I arch a brow, though "...why?"

"Because I'm willing to help in any way you need." Theo's response doesn't hold any hidden meaning, the expression on his face genuine. "I'm not looking for favors or control over you, pretty girl. Just for you to know I'm here in any capacity you need. You can't kill me, nothing can, but I'd let you practice on me either way."

"You're serious?" I ask, my heart fluttering wildly inside my chest. His trust in me is humbling.

"I am."

Shifting back a smidge so I can meet his stare a little better, I ignore the slight growl of protest that builds in his throat and smile. "That's sweet you'd let me kill you, but I couldn't even if I wanted to. You're going to be stuck with me for a long time."

Always. No way out for either of us.

"I'd never stop you from trying, Gabriella." The way he says my name with reverence—the deep timbre with a velvet quality—sends a delicious rush of excitement through every limb. He knows the way he affects me; I see the way his mouth curves up into a sly grin, and I can't help but to match it. *How can a man I just met become my world within the span of a few hours?* Because he has. Totally and irrevocably.

"Are you daring me to, Theo? Want to play with me?"

"Always." Those beautiful eyes flash red for a second, the truth of his nature winking at me. Vampires are known to be volatile and unreasonable—impulsive—and yet their king is wrapped around me like a warm blanket, the rumbling in his chest a secret song just for me. *Why does he feel human to me?* "Just know I'll always come back to you."

"You have no choice."

"I'm a demon, sweetheart. Can't kill what's never truly been alive."

My brows furrow. *What does that even mean?*

Then again, there's so much we don't know about each other:

Likes and dislikes.

How we grew up.

Our dreams for the future.

How his body temperature mimics mine while his flesh molds to me when it should be hard. Unmovable. Cold.

Curiosity is a funny bitch and I blurt out my first question, much to his amusement. "How can that be, when I feel the rise and fall of your chest? Your every exhale is a caress across my skin."

"My father is a demon, while my mother was a human," he answers me as if that explains everything. It doesn't. Instead, I'm left with more inquiries than before. I also don't miss how he refers to one parent as being alive while the other as passed.

"Then you *are* half-human?" *I thought all vampires were made, not born.*

"I'm not." Theodore moves us, pulling me with him to sit before I can argue. We kneel on his bed, the mattress sinking a bit under our combined weight while we face each other. Our knees touch. Our chests rise and fall in sync. "Pay attention."

"What're you..." I trail off on a hiss, watching with wide eyes as the extended nail of his pointer finger trails across my left breast, an inch above the edge of my dress. A shallow cut, just large enough that a few rivulets of blood pour from the small wound. My complaint ceases at that, though, because now I'm transfixed by the similar sharp line he drags across his chest.

This one is deeper. His claw slices through the hard flesh as if it were churned cream, and as morbid as the sight is, I find myself leaning closer. There's blood at the wound, which contradicts his non-human argument, but when I look a little closer, I notice the difference. While my sanguine drops are a bright red and thin in consistency, his are thick and darker—almost the color of dried blood. The beads fall like mine, slowly, but the distinction is clear to see.

But then again, I've never heard of a vampire bleeding.

Or being warm. Or breathing. *What the heck?*

They take, feast on the life source of all living creatures, and yet their veins remain dry.

"You see it." My response is a nod, my eyes held by the sight.

"My father is connected to the underworld, pretty girl. He's a god—a very powerful one—and before most of creation was past its primitive stage, he took a small reprieve from his duty."

"A god?"

"Yes."

"And he came here?"

"He did." His large hands cup my face, and each sweep of his fingertips across my cheeks brings goose bumps to my sensitive skin. But then again, all of me feels this way. Raw, exposed, and his. It's unlike any feeling I've encountered in my twenty summers; all-encompassing and rooted so deep within my soul that I feel him all around me.

A part of me. We are one.

"Was your mother fully human?"

Theo nods, and I'm a bit surprised by the hint of sadness in his expression. "A chief's daughter with no real knowledge of what he was. My father took her from her home, got her pregnant, and stayed until the day of my birth a few months later."

"And she's—"

"I killed her."

"What?" The ease with which he admits this causes me to jerk back. "You killed her?"

"I drained her from within before tearing through her abdomen." Another caress, his eyes flashing red as they watch a vein in my neck tick. "I'm a monster, sweetheart. No part of me has or will ever be human."

"What you *are* is perfect for me." The words slip before I can register, but the truth is there nonetheless. Theodore didn't ask to be created from the union, nor did he have control over his needs. He fed. "You also did what all babies do, Theo. They feed on the breasts of their mothers and find sustenance in what they can provide. You were just a bit different."

"You're extraordinary. So fucking beautiful." That is all he says, but his true emotions are there in his eyes. Still red, bright, and unyielding in his stare, but they show his truth. This bone-deep senti-ment that I return without conscious thought, my small hand now cradling his sharp jaw with just the right amount of facial hair, a sexy stubble I find myself wanting to feel rubbing against my thighs.

My thoughts are all over the place.

Surprise. Happiness. Shock. Lust.

They're tumultuous and uncontrollable, taking me from one frantic extreme to the other all within the span of a single breath.

"This is crazy." Without conscious thought, I bring my face closer to his. He watches me do so, his nostrils flaring a bit when a small trickle of excitement coats the pink flesh between my thighs and nipples tighten to stiff peaks.

"Yet you want it. Want me." Denying our mate bond is a slap in the face to the one belief every species obeys. There's one soul meant to bind with yours. One heart that will share the same beat, and while Theo's technically doesn't, I still hear it. It's low and steady; a *thump thump thump* that sings only to me.

"I do." Closer, and I can almost taste him in the air between us. "Will never deny you."

"Then kiss me."

"Is that a request?"

"No." His body moves slightly closer while his hands grip my hips. "I'm commanding you to."

"And who am I to disappoint a king." The moment our lips touch, I let out a breathy sigh. Theo's lips are soft and plump, the fullness making me itch to bite them, and I do, embedding my teeth in deep while his chest vibrates. While those strong hands hold me a little tighter within his hold.

Then, there's the sound of fabric stretching—the protest loud inside the quiet room where only my harsh breaths can be heard.

"I need to feel you." He fists a little more and the slits at my sides ride higher, exposing flesh to the fresh air. Theodore's nostrils flare and his sharp fangs drop, tongue slicing across his bottom lip and then mine—tasting me. "Please, pretty girl. Nothing between us." This leaves him on a rumbled groan, those amber eyes turning bloody red within my next intake of breath. Bright. Heated. "Skin on skin."

"Yes." My dress is torn off before the last syllable passes through my lips. At once, my skin prickles with excitement and the goosebumps on my arms have nothing to do with the cool night's air.

I'm bare. On complete display.

The ruby of his eyes turns dark, almost black, yet the hint of red still reflects off the candles in the room. They're beautiful. Everything about him is.

Theodore's handsome with a sharp jaw, piercing stare, and dark hair. The epitome of tall, dark, and dangerous, yet, as I pull back for a second and stare, I see what others don't. There's more to him. More than the rumors and horror stories.

More to the beast.

He also doesn't like the fact I moved back. He's quick to hover over me, pushing me down toward the mattress, but before my body touches the plush bedding, I'm being lifted into a strong embrace and I wrap my legs around him without prompting.

My lips also twist into a sassy pout. "You don't want me to admire my mate?"

"After?" *Gods,* that deep voice will be my undoing. He brings out of me reactions and behaviors I've never experienced before. I want to flirt and giggle and spread my legs a little wider. *I'm going to become a whore for this man.* "First, I need another taste."

"Taste of what?"

"You." Before I can ask for clarification, I'm being kissed. This one is hungrier than the last and I'm being swept away by the lust and need he creates, arching into him as my hands rise to cup the back of his head, fingers fisting the short strands. One sharp tug, and he growls into my mouth. I also notice that his fangs have retracted, and a part of me is sad because of it.

I want to feel them again. To lick them. No part of me is shy when it comes to the man holding me, pressing my bare core against the front of his pants where I know there'll be proof of my desire left behind.

Dragging his teeth down my lip, he flicks the tip of his tongue there and I feel it at my core, causing me to clench. To angle my head a little more to the side so I can try to recapture his mouth, yet he denies me, choosing instead to travel a little lower to my chin and then the column of my throat where he inhales deep.

His exhales warm my skin as a sliver of fear runs through me.

Will he bite me?

Do I want to be so soon?

"Not yet," he hisses, nose sliding toward the vein that throbs in time with my racing heartbeat. Not in fear, but anticipation, and I melt under his tongue when he runs the tip from the underside of my jaw to my collarbone, loving the skin with nips and flicks—sucking until my hips buck up and I feel the drops of my wetness slide from my tiny hole to back entrance. "Motherfuck, sweetness. It's taking all that I am not to sink in deep; both my teeth and cock are aching to feel you shatter beneath me."

"Oh Gods," I moan, shaking when he pulls the skin right over the very top of my breast between his lips and sucks deeper, just shy of pain, and then releases the abused flesh.

Theo lifts his beautiful face, eyes dark and hungry, to admire his work. "Beautiful."

"Yours."

"That's right. You are." Dark orbs travel lower, grazing my painfully hard nipples and then the flat of my stomach before settling on the small triangle of curls above where I'm needy the most. His snarl is loud inside the room, his body shaking violently, yet he doesn't pull away. Instead, he brings one hand to my throat and the other to my mound, tracing two fingers across the soft hair. "Who did you do this for?"

"W-what?" I ask, voice shaky at his actions yet turned on just the same. "What do you mean?"

"Where's the rest, pretty girl? Why are your lips bare?"

"I don't like it."

"Keep talking." The warm digit moves down a bit, just over my clit, and my walls clench and thighs tremble as a shock of pleasure slams into me without warning. It feels good. Too good. "Why are you nearly bare?"

Goose bumps rise on my skin at his dark tone. "My mother taught us to remove unwanted hair with a sugar wax recipe that's natural and easy to make."

"Continue?" More relaxed now, yet the two fingers running down to my labia and up again remain firm. His hand on my throat tightens a tiny bit.

"And I decided to try it one day since I've always hated the hair there. It's annoying, to be honest." My nipples throb, the closeness of his mouth to my body causing an involuntary mewl to slip. Seeing this, Theo lowers his face to hover just over my left breast, his exhale making the fire rising within my veins worse. He doesn't, but instead arches a brow. A silent demand that I finish my explanation. "It was different from doing my legs or underarms, but I was able to remove it and leave myself bare except for the small patch you see. It also keeps me this way for about three weeks."

"Hmm." That's his response, but then it doesn't matter as his mouth takes a nipple into his mouth and pulls it between his teeth. The pain registers quickly, but it's mixed with pleasure as he pinches my clit, causing my body to try and bow into itself. I'm arching and squirming and then trying to pull back, the latter of which pisses him off, and I'm rewarded by an angry growl. "Don't."

"Theo, I—"

"Just feel, pretty girl. Let me enjoy you." Not that I'm given a chance to catch up. His mouth descends on my breast, licking and sucking from one side to the other, and right when I'm going to voice my need for more—for another taste of his teeth—he bites the right tip and then the underside, digging a little harder there. *Another mark.*

The fingers on my pussy massage my clit in time with every nip that follows, while the hand on my throat is tight. Neither moves when he repositions himself between my legs and licks a trail from my sternum to belly button before stopping just above my mound.

I follow his every move.

Watch as his fangs descend right before he nuzzles the small patch of hair, breathing me in deep.

Theodore stays there for a moment, and I don't move. Can't. I'm too enraptured by the sight.

However, a few seconds later I'm crying out. There's a slight sting near my labia, a fiery throb that's unexpected right before my eyes roll back and the world disappears.

He's licking me there. Right over my clit, and the pain quickly turns into bliss. Each stroke of his tongue leaves me breathless, fighting his hold to move against his mouth that promises nirvana.

At the first undulation of my hips, his head snaps up, though. There's anger in those eyes, glaring at me, but I'm frozen by something else. There's blood on his lips, smeared across and down his chin, and maybe I'm sick because I find it sexy.

The sight. The hunger staring back at me.

Him.

"Don't move." His teeth are clenched, fangs out with a few drops of red falling from the tip. My body spasms at the sight, shivers at the resurfacing of aches where he cut me—the sting coming from the area between my lip and the crease of my left thigh. "I'm tempting fate enough today."

"Theo, please. It hurts."

"My poor baby," he coos, the fingers on my throat flexing. "So needy. Such a pretty little cunt." The vulgarity in that one word only heightens my arousal, and the proof slips from my clenching hole. Not that he lets a single drop get far, his mouth slanting over my slit while his tongue laps—devours me.

I'm left clinging to the bedsheets below while hovering on a dangerous edge with no rope.

This is unlike anything I've ever experienced. My hand has never made me feel delirious—weightless—while a tidal wave of ecstasy threatens to bury me in its wrath.

And yet as it looms, I can't look away.

Not when he's watching my reactions. Not when his tongue laps near the cut, not touching directly, but I know he's drinking from me.

Another heady experience.

To know I'm his sustenance. I'll satiate his thirst.

"More." A demand from me. A plea.

"Louder."

"Theo, I need...oh *fuck*!" I scream the latter, my entire body tightening when his fingers connect with my outer thigh a second time. Between his nips and licks and now the slight prick of pain, I'm on overload. Almost there. My eyes become glassy with unshed tears; I'm racked with shivers beneath him. "More."

"Feed me." Two words. That's what equates to my utter and total destruction, but when the flat of his tongue runs from my entrance to clit, a near featherlight touch, I come. A euphoric sensation slams into me and I arch back despite his hold on me, losing myself to the experience.

"That's my pretty girl." His praise feels like glory, and more so when he continues his assault through each pulse. My muscles lock and core clenches, the wave a never-ending torrent of beautiful pain under his tongue and hold.

And only when the last bit of pleasure is wrung from my body does he release my neck and then licks the aching wound his fangs created. It hurts a bit when he does, but that soon numbs and I'm left a jittery, smiling mess atop his covers.

A very sleepy mess at that.

"You wore me out," I hear myself say, but things are slowing down around me now. My eyes are closing, noises ebbing, and the last thing I make out is his warm chuckle before it all goes black.

Vampire King
THEODORE
ASTOR

We've been inside my private quarters for three days now, and we've yet to do two things:

Discuss why she came. Consummate the bond.

Both are important, yet the latter will have to wait a tiny bit.

I want to surprise her. Spoil her.

However, she's restless today, and I have something that will help.

Gabriella needs answers. To learn the truth.

I'll give that to her today.

Nuzzling her cheek, I lay a kiss on her jaw. "Time to get up, sleepyhead. I have a gift for you."

"Hmmm." That's all I get, accompanied by a noncommittal grunt as she tries to burrow deeper under the covers. It's a little after five in the evening, and those who work in the castle are up and getting their days started—making sure everything is ready for my mate.

Because my people know and are ready to receive their queen.

"You'll enjoy it."

"More sleep." Her beautiful face is a bit pinched, lips in a pout. "I'm not immortal."

At that, I throw my head back and laugh. The sound reverberates through the room, shaking the windows a bit. "I like you a little petulant. Bratty."

She cracks one eye open, glaring at me. "Sleeping is being bratty?"

"Anything you do without me is." Gripping the sheet over her, I lift it and crawl underneath. Like the predator I am, I hold myself above her, one hand to the left of her head while the other moves her hair back, exposing a long and graceful neck. The vein there thrums in time with her racing heart, yet it's the scent of her arousal that I'm most infatuated by.

It's sweet. Like cherries and fresh cream.

More so with her body bare and warm.

I breathe in deeply, and a rumbled groan of satisfaction builds in the back of my throat; it makes her shake a little, a whimper escaping, but I also don't miss the way her ass lifts up to present both holes to me.

Dirty little girl.

"Do you want a gift, or a reward?" Her heat sears me. Her pink pussy tempts me.

I want to sink in deep. To feel her body break under mine.

"How about you eat while I nap?" That earns Gabriella a quick smack to her right asscheek. The flesh bounces, lighting into a glowing pink where my fingerprints adorn her skin. "Hey!"

"Tempting offer, but later. Right now, I need you to get up and be ready in fifteen minutes."

"What's the rush? Are we going somewhere?" My pretty girl sits up and I let her, moving back just enough so she can turn and get comfortable. "Is everything okay?"

I nod, my mouth lifting into a grin. "I have a present for you."

Her perfectly sculpted brow arches. "Not that I'm not grateful, Theo, but this couldn't wait another hour?"

"Do you wish to meet the man who killed your mother later?"

At once, the room grows colder, and hisses can be heard throughout my lands as vampires feel her anger—a wrath that pulsates between us, and it's because they've accepted her. They'll always have a bond with her. Obey her.

"Where?"

"In my dungeon."

"Take me to him." Not a request, but a demand as her ire morphs with her beauty, gifting me a tiny demon sprite. Small. Delicate. Lethal. "I'm owed his blood."

"Your wish is my command, my Queen."

HER SMALL HAND is in mine as we walk inside the tall tower that houses my prisoners and their guards. They're held below the ground while my men have dormitories in the upper levels, giving them a resting place when on duty that is occupied only by those on a specific shift.

The lower ones, however, are only accessible down a narrow set of stairs lit by an eternal flame gifted by an old mage seventy years ago that owed me a favor. I spared her cocky son, and she secured this structure.

"What the?" Gabby mutters under her breath, body visibly shaking as we enter the lowest level. I'm not going to deny the smell is unpleasant, the crying of those inside annoying, but I don't think that's quite what she's referring to. "Who did this?"

"She's long passed. Her name was Sylvanna Lastra."

"What she was is sloppy." Tone a little abrasive, she purses her lips. "The energy isn't concentrated; it's flickering and weak. An unattended spell can be volatile, and not to be rude, but useless."

"Someone's snobby about her magic."

Gabriella bristles at the jab, but her lips twitch just the same. "I am. Won't deny it."

"Does that mean you'll be inspecting every corner of our kingdom, love?" A snort escapes her, and fuck me if I don't find that utterly adorable. *What she does to me. I'm wrapped around her finger.* "That you want to protect your people."

"I always want my people protected. That's why I came to you not knowing who you are to me."

Stopping abruptly, I pin her against the nearest wall with my body, not an inch of space between us. "And what am I to you?"

Her gasps are sweet. The way those green eyes darken is a weakness. "You're mine."

"Always."

"Good." Caging my face with her hands, she places her lips over mine, just breathing me in. "Now, after we handle whatever is needed today…we need to talk. My protection is now extended to you and yours, and while you probably don't need it, it's there just the same. Please don't fight me on that."

"I'd never. To me, it's an honor."

"Good boy," she coos, and I hiss, baring my fangs. She's not afraid; I scent her arousal. "Not that I'm giving you much of a choice in this. I'm very stubborn, King Astor. You might as well accept that now, save you many frustrations down the line."

"How do you figure that?"

"Happy wife. Happy life." Her shrug is nonchalant. "It's what my father always said."

"You Wiccans and your ideologies." I drag my teeth down her chin. Nip the skin there.

"Want to test that theory, Theo?" Gabriella arches her neck, thrusting her chest against mine. Giving me more room. "Need a demonstration, maybe?"

"No." Instead, I attack the fragrant skin with gentle bites and open-mouthed kisses. From right to left, I make sure she's marked for all to see.

"Smart man." A whimper. "You'll make a fine mate."

Spinning us around, I secure one hand beneath her ass and lift, wrapping her thighs around my waist. The other hand makes contact with her asscheek. The sound is loud, but she doesn't cry out. Instead, the smarting smack causes the woman in my arms to moan low, a throaty sound that settles on the tip of my dick while a bead of pre-come slides down from the slit on the head.

I do it again. Three more times on the same spot so I know she'll feel me later.

"You're making it hard for me to serve justice on a silver platter, sweetheart." All crying around us has ceased, those inside of the prisons listening intently. Not that I give a fuck. I'd kill them all after pleasing my girl. "That smart mouth of yours is dangerous, for me and you, and the only thing I want right now is to bend you over this railing so everyone below us can hear you scream."

"Maybe after?"

"Think you're ready for me?"

"Born to be yours." Four words, her honesty, is my undoing, and I kiss her, slowly and full of every bit of the emotions she evokes in me. It's caring and soft and the opposite of who I am as a demon, and yet I'm hers.

My world revolves around her. I bend the knee for her.

She humbles me.

"Thank you." Slowing the kiss, I flick the tip of her tongue with mine and then pull back. "Ready to confront him?"

Immediately, the heady lust blanketing us chills and her expression turns cold. Full of anger. "Yes."

"Stay close." Placing her down, I retake her hand and pull her behind me. We take the remaining stairs, the silence looming as those inside cells know I'm the one making the rounds. None stand close to the door. None investigate. Instead, I see the huddled forms in corners with their knees bent and faces turned away, avoiding direct interaction.

On the last step, I turn to the left and toward the two doors there. One is occupied permanently, and the other has a man who's only inside for accessibility reasons and will go back to his room on my property right after this little chat.

He will leave in the morning a rich man.

The heartbeats behind the metal doors beat fast.

There are two guards standing outside each cell, too, waiting with their eyes straight ahead. Once we stop, we both place a hand on the handle and pull, exposing the people within.

The patriarch of the Rossi family.

The representative of the Mariano family.

One in chains, while the other sits on a chair with a small table in front of him. Their heads snap in our direction, and it's Mariano who seems deathly afraid.

"Nicolo?" A palpable chill fills the space, while the hand gripping mine tightens and I feel this concentrated vibration at her palm. "You did this? You killed my mother?"

"Gabriella, I swear I didn't." Both his pale hands go up. "I'm here for information King Astor needed. That's it."

"Under what benefit?"

"My wife and sister—"

"Where are they?" my mate spits, her hard eye flicking to me. She's like an angry kitten; I just want to lay us down on my bed and pet her. "Who has them and the child?"

"They've been sent to the Moore home. Should be there now, or arriving soon." At my assurance to her, the stiffness—bouncing knee —in Nicolo calms and he lets out a rough exhale. "My word is law."

"And what was the agreement?" Gabriella asks, yet her eyes are on the older Rossi. The pain in her expression cuts me, my chest— my dead heart—throbs and it's an uncomfortable sensation.

I've never experienced this before.

The emotional hurt.

The sadness.

All foreign, and I don't like them. How they affect her.

"I'd testify against those that rose up against your family." Nicolo moves to stand, but the look in my eye makes him abandon the thought quickly. "Tomasso Mariano and his mother were approached by another king while his father was still alive. The monarch offered them a higher rank—control over all witches—if they pledged their loyalty and helped remove King Paolo."

Mariano's brother-in-law takes a breath, his anxiety high. His fear is a delicious scent in the room; it overpowers all others.

"Continue, but Nicolo…" Releasing my hand, Gabby walks to the doorway of his cell and stares. Her eyes are hard. "I want names. Who's the king?"

"Don't you fucking answer, you traitor," Rossi snaps, fighting against his binds. The scent of blood soon permeates the air and my guards hiss, their muscles coiling to attack. "Stay quiet, or I'll slit your throat myself."

I'm in front of Rossi before the last word passes his lips, yet it's not necessary for me to lift a hand. His face begins to turn red, neck straining while his lips mouth a useless prayer. He pleads with me of all beings.

Fucking waste of space.

"Talk. Don't make me hurt you." Her words, the dark edge in her tone, are an aphrodisiac to my senses. Because there's evil in every-one, but it's hers I want to experience.

Burn in it. Feast on it.

"King Larue." *That conniving son of a bitch.*

"The faes are behind this mess? Are you sure?" A little calmer, she asks this while the older man still struggles to breathe. It's as if his life force is being taken from him a second at a time. His eyeless form has grown pallid, seems to have become thinner. "Please be certain as once I act, there will be no going back."

"I overheard Lilibeth and Tomasso in his office after coming home late one evening." Nico swallows hard, shame dominating his features. "I'd taken my wife, sister, and niece out for a meal, but halfway there realized my wallet was atop my dresser. After rushing inside to get it, I walked in on the tail end of their conversation and tryst; she was on her knees praising him for the arrangements made with the king. They would take the crown, another woman would join with King Astor, and both would work together to eradicate the wolves after pledging loyalty to Larue."

He's already told me as much, and I'm not impressed by the idiocy presented as a plan. I've never been a man to be led by my cock, my partners in the past meant shit, and the one who could damage me isn't the type.

My mate doesn't care for power.

She exudes it without trying. Holds more than most and was below me until we crossed paths. Now, though, she's *the* apex.

I do her bidding.

"How long have you known?"

"I should've spoken sooner."

"Yes. You should have." A scream rends the air and I'm over to them in an instant, walking inside just as she tosses his tongue to the floor, his blood dripping from the knife I recognize from our first meeting. She's gripping the handle tight, fingers turning white from exertion. "This is my punishment for you, Nicolo. Had you used that appendage, been strong and full of honor, my parents could've been saved. Your silence is now infinite; be thankful that's all I take." Turning to face me, she smiles. "Please send him back to his family. He's learned his lesson."

"As you wish." With the snap of my fingers, both guards look up, pride in their eyes while Nico whimpers—crying in a heap on the ground. The one to the left is one of my generals, and he awaits orders while the other stands at position; he'll clean up what is left behind. No trace will be accepted. "Brodej, he's to be escorted and remain unharmed. I want three men with him, and then they are to stay and guard the Moore borders until we decide how to proceed.

No one in or out unless Paolo's children grant permission. Is that understood?"

"Yes, my lord. Would you like me to accompany him?"

"Not yet, but I expect those you choose to be discreet and trustworthy."

"Yes, your majesties." Not just me. He addresses her too, and the flash of softness in her eyes toward him is proof she heard. "No harm shall come to them."

"Thank you, Brodej." Gabriella walks over, placing herself in front of me, and gives him a curtsy. My general is old. He's seen a lot of the world as the head of my army, his position slightly above Veltross, and manners is the one thing he appreciates after integrity. It shows respect —acceptance—and coming from his queen, that's a valuable honor. "When you reach my lands, please ask for Augusto and say the words *by blood and pact* and he will reply *we are one*. That promise is sacred to us, and no one outside of those we trust know it. He'll know I sent you."

"It will be done, my queen." A moment later he walks out of the cell occupied with Nicolo, the man leaning heavily on him, and they disappear up the stairs. Quiet once again fills the room, yet this time the acrid scent of piss is heavy. Fresh.

"That's gross."

"Agreed, pretty girl." Without being asked, the other guard rushes over to an old well at the center of the room and brings up a deep bucket of water, the liquid sloshing over the sides before it splashes the old fool. Rossi coughs, his chest sounding rough, yet his color has returned to normal.

No longer choking. Gabriella relaxed her control over him.

That is, until she turns in his direction. There's darkness in her eyes. The need for revenge. "Why?"

"Gabriella, he's poisoning you against your people. How could you believe that I'd ever...*fuck!*" His body thrashes, mouth open in a scream loud enough that those on the other floors whimper. I hear their prayer for leniency—not for him, but themselves—and then the pacing of another. Chains scrape against the floor from one side to the other, and I smirk.

He's a defiant soul, and yet to have an audience with me.

I've kept him for my own amusement.

A trespasser on my land that was dumb enough to get caught.

I'll let him rot for a century before granting him an audience.

"Answer me," my pretty girl says, her voice calm. Too calm. Yet her hands are fisted, her wrists moving in circular patterns and with each rotation, Rossi further cries out in pain. "Be a man and face me."

"You don't demand from me, cunt." He's crying, the words gritted out, yet when Gabby snaps one hand to the left, the sound that rends the air is that of a broken bone. From the sound of it, it's in the area of his spine, and after he still refuses to answer, she smirks and the right hand mimics her earlier action.

Blood pours from his nose and empty eye socket. More fractures.

"Mori in igne." No sooner have the words passed through her plump lips than the room heats and his bones expand, pushing against his flesh without an exit. The skin stretches, bruises rising from deep within while his entire frame shakes from the pain.

Die in fire.

Such a simple command, but the effect is a beautiful thing to witness. To see a grown man crumble like a pathetic bitch.

"Please stop."

"Beg me." Her hands open and he slumps, head lolling. Her alluring green eyes look at me and she tilts her head in his direction, the silent request clear. "Go on, Mr. Rossi. Beg."

Only garbled groans are heard from him, and that won't do. In two strides I'm standing in his direct line of sight, and on his next intake of breath, my hand smacks him across the face. His head snaps to the side and his front teeth break, the bloodied nose now a small geyser and it sprays me, ruining my shirt and dirtying my face.

I want to sink my teeth into his neck and rip it out, laying it at her feet like a present.

But I don't. He's hers to kill. I'll never take that away from her for two reasons.

His actions hurt her.

And secondly, I find her powers and thirst for blood deliciously sinful. The best kind of foreplay.

"The next time she asks and you deny her, I'll rip off one limb. Deny her after that, and I'll make you eat it."

"Why are you helping her? She's beneath—"

"My mate is above all. Even me." Reality sinks in then. There is no way out. "Answer her."

"With my daughter as queen, I would've had a seat of power over our kind." Low, so low and meek. "Tomasso was willing to forfeit his wife and keep her as a concubine and my daughter would do the same; her human mate would've been a pet. The offer was too tempting and your father too stupid—too trusting to see the seeds of revolt we planted. It wasn't personal, Gabriella. Paolo just had what we wanted."

"You sick son of a bitch." Nothing else, and I watch in amazement as her eyes flash brighter, the green almost neon, before his desperate cries fill the room. The curses and pleas all meld together while her body crouches and hands lay flat on the ground. An incantation almost too low for me to understand flows from her lips, but the more she whispers, the more he screams.

"*Mortem.*"

His blood flows down from cuts that a second ago were not there and he slowly becomes emaciated, sucked into himself until nothing is left of the arrogant man but hollow features and flaky skin.

Motherfucking beautiful.

"May he rot in the afterlife."

"He will." Of that I have no doubt. My father will see to it.

"Thank you." Turning toward me, my mate takes the steps between us and stands up on the tip of her toes, barely reaching my lips. Not that she kisses me. Instead, the minx nips my jaw and then lowers herself with a shy look. *How could she still look so innocent after doing what she did?* But fuck me if I don't love it. "I have one more request, and I'd like to spend some time with you outdoors. Just us."

"Ask me."

"I want to meet your coven."

"It would be an honor."

Vampire King
THEODORE ASTOR

We leave the prison and I walk us with my hand on the small of her back, passing by a few important wings of the castle. I promise to give her a personal tour later, but right now I want to take her somewhere I think she'd enjoy.

Witches love nature.

They feed off the earth while giving back, and a large part of nature is the animal kingdom. The circle of life is a unique one, simple, and one many don't respect like her kind does. I also know she needs to be outside and not always cooped up in our room. Her petite body needs to cleanse her soul with fresh air and rest—truly rest—near what she holds sacred.

So we walk in silence through the halls, and many who are rushing around know better than to look. They're preparing for the announcement tonight; we pass the opulent décor and move toward a large area of untouched land far from the cliff's edge with a drop onto the surrounding sea.

The closer we get, the more our bond thrums with contentment—she's excited.

The simple dress she's wearing is similar to the one she wore the day we met; I had the palace's personal seamstress replicate the form-fitting, tight silhouette with a lower neckline. Just a bit. The black color complements her skin with a slight golden hue from hours outside and the fiery waves that flow down her back. This cut spells wicked trouble.

Emerald eyes complete her ethereal look; Gabriella is a natural beauty, and mine. All motherfucking mine.

I might be a possessive bastard, but I'm not going to stop her from being who she is.

An unintentional tease. Provocative.

Coquettish without trying.

I'll just kill anyone who lusts over what's mine. Simple as.

The gate to my sanctuary is large and ornate, the metal creaking a bit as I push it open and step through, my hand guiding her forward. And it's when the low snarl of a large cat greets her ears that she pauses.

"What is this place?" she asks, her smile wide and expression curious, more so when a large flock of birds flies overhead, as if spooked.

"This is my private zoo, pretty girl."

"A zoo? Are you serious?" Her eyebrows shoot up to almost her hairline, and I once again find myself chuckling—relaxing.

How many times have I done so since meeting her? It's natural, though.

How can it not be when she's the best part of me?

But more importantly, it cements how foolish I've been in the past regarding mates.

I would never trade what we have. Our bond. Our future.

"Very much so." Rustling in a bush to the right of us catches our attention, and her head turns while I watch *her*. Gabriella doesn't disappoint; she takes a step back into me—hand darting to grasp my arm while the neat blunt edge of her nails tries to dig into my skin. I'm even impressed with the minute sting that accompanies it; she shouldn't be able to inflict any kind of pain. "Don't move."

A large, white albino snake slithers from the greenery with a man's neck caught between its teeth. The male's unconscious, body limp, but what catches my attention is his scent.

He's fae. Royal blood.

"Holy shit." Pretty girl's whisper-yell makes the snake tilt its head, a slightly amused curl of the lip while the body is dropped a few feet from us. Seconds pass before the animal coils, its head waiting for orders. "What is a fae doing here?"

"That's what you're surprised by?"

Green eyes flicker to me, her head nodding. "Aren't you?"

"Not the animal?"

"He's one of yours. You'd have attacked otherwise." Not a question, and she's right. Hell, had Tero come any closer, I would've hurt him. "Is he a pet, or…?"

"Shifter. And yes, he's loyal."

"Good. Then I won't scream." A hiss-like sound comes from the beast, a laugh, and Gabby gives him a look. Just one; serious and with eyes narrowed, and the snakes swallows hard. "Don't get cocky. I'm still considering bopping you on the nose for the less-than-stellar warning. Snakes freak me out."

Tero's head lowers even more, coils tighter. Admonished.

He looks pitiful and gives us the equivalent of a wounded puppy look. *What the fuck?*

"Are you alone?" I ask then, and both look over at me. Tero's head nods, head tilting to the side in silent question as if saying *where do you want him?* "Take him down to level two, and if anything is on him—weapon or otherwise—place it atop my desk. We'll be back late."

The animal turns his head and moves to pick up the unconscious man, but Gabby steps forward, causing him to pause. Tero freezes as she takes the steps between them and extends a hand, placing the warm palm on his head. She's not petting him but reading his aura—I've seen her father do it while alive—and his eyes close, the pastel shade of blue lighting to an almost translucent color.

This takes no more than a second, but when she pulls back, Tero's in the most peaceful trance I've ever seen. Languid, he lays right where he is. His breathing is deep and even, but not asleep.

"I like him." Pretty girl looks at me from over her shoulder, her body language matching his. Loose. A little drunk. "His intentions are honest, and his heart is loyal. He's thankful to you. Whatever you did to gain his trust, it's for life. His kind are straightforward that way."

"You know of his kind?"

"All magical creatures are studied by the elders of our clan. My grandmother, while alive, was one of them, and she had a friend who was serpentine, a coral shifter."

"And she displayed the same character traits as Tero?"

"Yes. They all do, but—"

"But?"

"Make an enemy of one, and you've signed a death warrant."

"Good to know." Not that I don't trust him. He and his sister have been by my side for years, always willing to help—make sure my instructions are carried to the letter—since I brought them to live with me. I might be an asshole, but something within the young shifters when I met them resonated with me.

Maybe it was the fact they were alone, that their parents died during an attack of their village.

Maybe it was the fact he asked for nothing more than food and shelter for his sister. Not him. He would've been content to sleep outside as long as Marcia was protected.

"Come. Let's give him time to snap out of it," Gabriella speaks lowly, her hand reaching for mine, fingers intertwining. "Show me what you want me to see. I'm ready."

"Ready, or impatient?"

"Now who's the brat?" At her sassy response, I throw my head back and laugh, a deep, from-the-gut roar that causes her to giggle. It also gives me the opening I need, and when she brings a hand to her face and wipes under her eyes, I toss the little witch over my shoulder.

At first she yelps, caught off guard by the sudden move, but that soon morphs into a more playful side of her.

Her tiny hand smacks my ass.

Not once. Not twice.

Gabriella Moore does not stop until we reach the wide-open space where I have three big cats, and each is a different species: a jaguar, a cougar, and a tiger. Once the gate is closed behind me, I lower her to the ground, making sure that her body rubs against my front, pausing when her pussy presses against my hard cock.

That, I enjoy with a slow punch of my hips, and I'm rewarded by the sounds of her whimper.

My pretty girl.

The cats come close to us from different directions; they're picking up her scent and wanting to investigate. With my keen eyesight, I see the tiger first who's crouched down and working his way over. His whiskers twitch and body drags along the high grass. He's confused between wanting to pounce or run away.

I'm the larger predator.

You don't bite the hand that feeds.

Turning her around, I place her back to my front while wrapping an arm around her waist. "Do you see him?"

"Which one?"

"Good girl." She's aware of her surroundings.

"Do you see—"

"I feel them. There's three animals nearby, watching us." A dainty hand points in the direction of the tiger before flicking to the right. "Two are close, but the third I'm having a hard time pinpointing."

"That's because you're looking toward the group. Look up, pretty girl." Gabby leans her head back against my chest while surveying the trees nearby. For the most part, these big cats don't interact much, but curiosity—my presence—is pulling them in. My scent is one they know—I've raised them as a pastime—and as such come to wrestle and train.

Their bites and claws don't affect me. Yet, they know better than to test that limit.

"Found it," she exclaims after a few minutes, having noticed the jaguar up high and looking straight at her. He's the smartest of the three, more cunning. "Male or female?"

"Male."

"All of them?"

"Yes."

"That won't do." The tiger moves into striking position, but a sharp whistle makes him stop. They all do. "The heck?"

"You want me to get females for them?"

"Yes, but what was that?"

All three move into place not far from us and side by side. Another whistle and they sit on their haunches, a grumpy sound coming from the backs of their throats. Their eyes are also on me now. They've learned to follow each of my commands without hesitation.

"That's me reminding them to mind their manners." I bop her nose, then drag the tip of my finger down and over her lips. "You're not lunch."

"Am I not tasty?" The cheekiness in her is something I'm finding myself quite fond of. Something I would hate from anyone else.

"You're an aphrodisiac, sweetheart. But more importantly..." bringing my lips down to her ear, I exhale roughly against her skin and enjoy the quick rise of goose bumps there "...I don't share."

"Neither do I."

"Good girl." I walk us forward, her body still in my tight hold while the animals watch. They're not the only ones either; I have exotic birds, hippos, a rhino, and three cows just because. "Ready to meet these three knuckleheads?"

"How is this even real? Are they not afraid of you?"

"They are, but I rescued them from poachers as cubs and raised them. Different times, but always the same story."

"Money?" she asks, sadness in her tone.

"Yes, love. Money."

"You're not what I thought you'd be, you know?" Low, Gabriella says this so low I almost miss it. "In my head, you were this larger-than-life monster with no heart or remorse, and here you are rescuing animals and—"

"I'm not a saint."

"I know, but I hated you unjustly just the same." Won't deny that stings; a small laceration spreads across the area where my heart should be. Gabriella must sense this because she quickly turns in my arms and cages my face in her small hands, pulling me down to her. "That was on me, Theo. Not you." A small press of her mouth to mine releases every bit of the tension her confession brought on. "I put something on your shoulders that had no place being there, and I'm truly sorry. A man my father respects as much as he does—who my mother defends so adamantly—must have a good soul. Not perfect, but good."

"Your parents spoke of me to you?"

Gabby nods before giving me another peck. "The night we met, I dreamt with them."

"And they didn't tell you to run?"

"No. They told me to hold on tight." So many questions run through my mind at that, but before I can probe further, the cougar lets out a low growl. Her smile widens and she turns, retaking her place with her back against my chest. *Fuck, she feels good against me.* "I promise to explain everything to you, my gift and guilt, but I want to enjoy this with you first. I've never seen such animals up close."

I don't want that for her. To feel upset by something she had her reasons to feel.

My plans before finding her to be my mate weren't good.

I'd been planning to make her nothing more than a pet. My personal slave.

"Never apologize to me, Gabriella. My intentions with you weren't always pure."

"Never tell me not to, Theodore." Another playful yowl, this time from the tiger. He's lying down on his side, half exposing his belly. "Besides, I did put a knife to your neck when we met. I'm not without fault. Although, according to my mother, women are always right."

"Is that so?"

"Yes, and I want to get closer to them. Can we?"

She's going to keep me on my toes. I re-wrap my arm around her waist while raising my unoccupied hand high into the air. The other two lie down as well. Eyes always on me.

"You need to teach me that. It's very cool."

"We have eternity, love. I'll show you anything you want."

"And we can get them girlfriends?"

"If it makes you happy."

"It would."

"Consider it done." With a slight nudge, I walk us the rest of the way until we stand just mere inches from the adult beasts, their noises growing louder the closer I get.

Animals have always fascinated me. They've evolved so much since my birth, morphing to adapt to their environments, and I've studied different species as a pastime. Now, though, I see the true purpose for my own fascination, and it has everything to do with the woman crouching and petting the oldest of the three.

The jaguar lies like a content house cat while she gushes over him. Her entire being vibrates with excitement and happiness, and more importantly, I vow to always keep her that way.

Vampire King
THEODORE ASTOR

I survey the room and all those inside: my generals, higher-ranking members of my army, and the elders who stand before my throne watching with high anticipation. They know. I'm not hiding her.

Murmurs fill the space, yet no one makes eye contact with me, their low conversations center around the purpose for this meeting and whom the woman could be. They know it's not someone from our coven or the neighboring ones, the many who bow to me as their lord and king. All are excited—*all* but Veltross.

He seems upset for some reason. His expression is pinched, and his eyes are hard while looking toward a woman to the left of where he stands and across the room. I can't fully see her from the half-hidden position, but the feminine features are hard to ignore, as is the fake tiara upon her head.

He has a daughter with a human. Not something I give two fucks about, but if she's his offspring, she has no business here. She is of no rank. Has no purpose in my court.

But then it doesn't matter as my mate enters the room and all noise ceases. All eyes are on the vision in red walking toward me, the jeweled-lined bustier cinching to show off her curves before the skirt flares out a bit, her signature slit over the right leg.

Her long hair hangs over in coquettish waves down the center of her back while a gold and onyx crown sits atop her head. That piece alone has many falling to one knee, the elders bowing with a fist over their chests.

That's the symbol left behind by my father for my mother. He isn't completely heartless and did care for the woman he cursed to die.

How could he ever hurt her?

I could never hurt my pretty girl. Anyone but Gabriella.

The closer she walks, the more take notice of her heartbeat—the fog of surprise giving way to what she is. A sorceress. My perfect witch.

Their eyes ping-pong back and forth, waiting for a reaction, but not Veltross, who steps forward and in her path. "What are you doing here? How did you get in?" he hisses, arm reaching for hers and I'm next to them in an instant, my fingers wrapping around his wrist and yanking back. I tighten my hold, my fangs bared. "My lord, she's a witch. Did you know this?" Those around us tense, their accusing eyes on my girl. Wrong move. "She has to be trick—"

"Silence." He freezes, the air of importance he carries with him disappearing beneath my glare. "Not another word, or I'll detach your head and let my animals use it as a chew toy."

"Calm down, love. I knew this could happen." Pretty girl takes the steps between us and places her hand over mine that's holding Veltross. Her fingers squeeze mine, silently asking me to hurt him a little more, and I'm proud of the fact, before tapping my wrist with her pointer finger. "Let him go. I'm sure he meant no harm. Isn't that right...?"

Veltross doesn't answer her and with a quick move of my hand, I yank his ring finger off. He hisses, eyes flashing red, but my chuckle settles him down. His entire body language goes lax, but I'm not done.

This type of disrespect will never be allowed.

Not to her. Not to me.

I break the remaining hand, tearing the cold—dead—flesh from joint and bones, tossing it to the center of the room's floor. Since he rose this hand against his queen, it's only fair he pays with it.

"Kneel." He's whimpering, trying to appear smaller, but I kick out his leg, forcing him down to the ground. There's no blood at the wound, but a black, almost tar-like substance bubbles to the surface while it begins to repair itself.

At this point, he'd have two choices. Reattach, or have the skin close around the wound and stay without the limb.

I'm only giving him one.

"My king, this is all a misunderstanding. I worry for you." The stench of bullshit surrounds him, an acrid scent that tickles my nose, and I narrow my eyes. Not that he meets them. Instead, Veltross focuses on the expensive flooring, body shaking in agony. That injury had to hurt. "Please forgive me for stepping out of line. I'm sure she's—"

"She's my mate and queen." Five words that force those who'd been standing all this time, wondering if the general is correct in his backward assumption, to drop to their knees. "Gabriella of the Moore house is above you. Above me." More silence, and then the faint sound of hushed cries create a humming cadence that makes me smile. "Are there any objections?"

"My king, are you aware she's a witch?"

"Your point, General Veltross? Or is it that you consider me an idiot?"

"Never, my lord. Please forgive me."

"Give him a chance, Theo. It's a shock, and will be the same when my people learn of this." They both speak in unison, but it's her remark that I focus on. It makes me smile, a genuine one, and a few gasp at the sight.

"To this degree?" I'm intrigued by the thought. How they will react. "Should I be concerned?"

"No. I'd never allow harm to come to you." The vehemence, the truth in those words, ring through the room and those present look up in wonder. The truth is slamming into the vampiric kingdom like a wrecking ball as all, no matter where in the world they are, will feel this moment. "That is my vow to you."

"I'd kill for you." To protect. Because someone pissed her off. Both are acceptable to me. "You will always come first. Will always be my priority."

Gabby's grin is saucy, the twinkle in her green eyes so enchanting. "Let him go, Theo. He's learned his lesson."

"Submit, or death."

"King Astor, please—"

"Submit or death, Veltross. There is no other choice."

"My loyalty will always be to the crown." In pain, he rights himself and draws the injured arm to his chest. His eyes are on her this time. The respect he's showing now makes me look over at Brodej and he nods, already knowing what I'm thinking. Something is off with Veltross. "All hail our queen. May she lead us toward prosperous paths and many victories."

"All hail the queen." The voices meld, the room vibrating with the echo of our people. "All hail the queen."

Brodej leaves the room while his wife moves closer to the woman Veltross was glaring at earlier. She'll be watching her while Brodej does a little digging for me.

Something isn't right.

I'll be paying close attention to them both.

The elders are the first to rise, coming closer to where we stand. Their posture is unintimidating, trying to appear submissive as to not scare Gabriella, but my pretty girl just smiles and extends a warm hand to Carlo, the older of the group.

"Your majesty, it's a pleasure to—"

"Call me Gabriella. You have my permission after your honest acceptance without doubting your king once." The man is surprised, but you can see the ease at which she makes him feel, the calm that infiltrates every single inch of the castle at her poise and gracious display. "Now, I'm starving here. When is dinner being served?"

No one responds. They're not sure how to, but me, I laugh. It rumbles up my chest and is loud, the eyes of all here on me as they take in their king so relaxed. Doing something so mundane.

"Only you, pretty girl," I say, my amusement reverberating throughout the room while Gabby shrugs, her tiny hand intertwining with mine. More of our subjects ease up. They even let out a snicker at the irony. She's won them over without trying. "Want to watch the monsters feed, or join?"

"You drink, and I chew."

"Deal."

I took her back to my quarters to change after that, choosing to pull her away before people could come and talk to her. Not yet. Not after the reactions of some, something the elders understood, and after a few more introductions with the group, they bid us goodbye and chose to prepare our meals in the formal dining room.

A show of respect to both.

They're not dumb. She's the Wiccan princess, the daughter of the strongest sorceress and warlock to have ruled their lands. Paolo and Leonora were not to be taken lightly and their demise took many hands—heads that I will serve my pretty girl on a golden platter.

After changing, we walk back hand in hand to the dining room, the halls clear of any lingering vampires. My warning earlier, Veltross's hand, still lays in the middle of the floor as a reminder. Rank or no rank, I will teach a lesson.

The severity lies in the infraction. How upset Gabriella is.

Not that she paid them any mind; her head is held high and her body lax beside mine as I pull out her chair and help her sit. My hand lingers on the soft skin of her neck before taking my own place at the head of the table.

"You look beautiful, Gabriella." A touch of pink blooms across the apple of her cheeks, and I want to nip her skin there. Just a tiny cut. A few drops of her blood will appease me more than whatever meal is going to be brought inside.

"Thank you, but it's—"

"I like you in my clothes." And I do. The long dress shirt she borrowed dwarfs her small frame, the bottom edge sitting a little below mid-thigh. The white material lays gently over the swell of her breasts, highlighting the lack of underwear—something I adore on her.

That need to be free. That almost bare cunt with just a neatly trimmed triangle of hair is a weakness.

"So, I can steal whatever I want?"

"Yes."

"Even the royal mantle?" *Fuck*, she's going to be the end of the monster many have tried to kill and all have failed. Because I can see the image she's painted vividly, the way the blood-red cloak would drape over her bare body while she sat in my chair, long legs crossed while her upper body arches for me.

Exposed and indecent. Mouthwatering.

"I demand that you do." A small giggle escapes her at that, lips parting to reply, but a knock at the door cuts off the response. I smirk. "Enter."

Two massive doors part and three of my elders, all women this time, walk inside with our meals. A dome-covered plate for her, and a man dressed in an expensive suit for me.

Gabriella looks over at him, brows furrowed. "He's evil."

"Most of my donors are. I enjoy killing my own heartless kind."

"You're not like him, Theo. He has no heart."

"And I do?"

"You do." Leaning over, she grips my chin in a tiny hand and squeezes. Demands my full attention which I give, staring into her soft, gem-like eyes. "Never say that again. Understood?" My nod is indulgent, and the women watching gasp—become nervous of my reaction. I'm volatile, an asshole, but never with her. It's impossible for me to do so. "This…" she says while turning a little to place her other hand over my chest "…is mine. I hear the cadence no one else can. I feel each pump in my veins, merging with my own in synchronization."

"All of me is yours." I nip her palm before placing my face in her hand again.

"Thank you." Our eyes stay connected for another minute before we sit back and a woman places the food in front of Gabriella, while mine is thrown beside my left leg and away from her.

The man whimpers, his body bruised, and several cuts wrap around the areas where his chains tore through the skin. The blood is fresh, the potent scent tickling my nose and my fangs descend, yet I don't eat.

Not yet.

An audible click is heard next as the elders exit, and I tilt my head in the direction of her plate. "Please eat, love."

"I will when you do." There's a stubborn set to her jaw as she says this, her brow raised. "With you or not at all."

"So demanding," I chastise playfully, while my hand fists the back of my meal's head, forcing it back in an uncomfortable angle. A yelp rends the air, and a scrawny hand tries to fight my hold, but a low growl from me and he stops, freezing in place. Even his crying is done in silence now. "Are you sure?"

She nods, lips twitching at the corners. I also don't miss the way she eyes my teeth, not in fear but desire. "I'm not afraid of your nature."

Her scent matches the words. This is arousing her.

"Maybe you should be."

"Still a no." Lifting the dome from her dish, she licks her lips while eyeing the butternut squash ravioli with hunger. However, the way her thighs squeeze under the table—the minute shift is unmistakable—is more than enough proof that she's feeling needy. Yearns for my touch. "My compliments to the kitchen staff and the hands who prepared this."

Those inside the kitchen pause their cleaning, as do the elders, their low *our pleasure* in unison meeting my ears a few seconds after. They're all busy with preparations for the party we're hosting in a few nights; the deep scrubbing after bleeding out a few donors—the storing of bottles with O negative for aging inside our temperature-controlled cellar—is messy work.

Its hospital-grade refrigeration can keep the sanguine beverage fresh until we decide to use it.

"They heard and are feeling happy to have pleased you."

More blushing. More of that tempting scent, and it's getting harder to not sink my teeth into her graceful flesh.

"First bite is yours." *Fuck me*. What a tempting offer.

"As you wish." It takes no effort to lift the asshole—he weighs no more than a feather—and I bring his neck to my lips. He's fighting in earnest now, his cries filling the room.

"Please stop! What are you people?"

"Do you know why you're my meal tonight?" I ask instead as the tip of my fang punctures his skin. Not deep, just enough that blood breaks the surface and streaks down the side of his neck. "What have you done to be brought before me?"

"I'm innocent."

"I don't like liars." The hand on his scalp tightens around the dirty blond strands, pulling until chunks tear clean off. "Now, I'll ask one last time. Why are you here?"

"I've killed someone." His heart races, chest caving as he struggles to get air into his lungs. He's panicking. "Two of them, actually."

"Who?" My nails extend a little more, slicing into his scalp. "Who did you kill?"

"My wife and six-month-old son." The words are so low that I almost miss them. There's no scent of guilt on him; his fear is of me and not what he's done. "I beat and strangled them because she found out that I'd stolen from her family. That my mistress is her father's secretary."

"You took two innocent lives?" Gabriella asks, her tone so full of disgust. Her anger is palpable. "You hurt a child? A poor defenseless baby and his mother to save yourself?"

"Yes, but—"

"This is karma, you worthless human."

"Human? What are you?"

"Your judge, jury, and executioner." My pretty girl approves, our bond thrumming, and I place my teeth over the vein in his neck. It pulses in time with the heaves of his chest, his body locked by fear.

"Please don't. I'll disappear…never do it again."

"No." I sink my fangs in and rip through veins and muscles, eyes on Gabriella as the rich metallic taste of his life essence fills my mouth. My moan and his horror-filled screams reverberate off the walls while his nails break, giving under the stone-like body with no bend.

Her sweet scent and his fear as I feed are pleasurable. No meal has ever satisfied me more, yet I know the day I change her, nothing will compare.

I want to fuck her tight body as I almost drain her.

Another pull and my eyes roll back. The feel of a small hand on my hair as I feed is glorious. She strokes my scalp with her neatly trimmed nails, then down to my temple and jaw. Each pass is erotic; my cock is hard and jerks behind the confines of my zipper.

The man quits jerking and his heart slows until it stops on the last pull, and what's in my hold is cold and pallid, his eye sunken in as if emaciated.

I may be a monster, but those without sin are off-limits. No real man hurts his loved ones, much less to save his own pathetic ass.

"May he rot in the underworld."

Tipping my head back on the chair, I run the tip of my tongue across a fang. "Agreed, but you also deserve to be punished. You haven't eaten."

"I will, but I need you to do me a favor first."

"Ask me anything."

"Push your chair back."

"As you wish." *She wants to eat on my lap. She doesn't care if I'm a bloody mess.* Another throbbing pulse shoots down to the tip of my dick and I groan, doing just that. My chair scrapes against the floor and turns a bit, giving her the access she requires.

"Thank you, *my King.*"

Vampire King
THEODORE ASTOR

"My pleasure…*fuck*. Pretty girl, what are you doing?"

She drops to her knees in front of me, the shirt riding up while nimble fingers undo the button of my pants. Each one is done slowly, grazing every bit of the new flesh she uncovers until my engorged flesh greets the air.

It flexes, the angry head glistening with a bead of pre-come while she stares, her breathing heavy. For a second, those green eyes flash to mine and her pupils are enlarged—lust heavy in them while she bites her bottom lip.

She wants this. To please me.

"I need to touch you." Such a simple truth and one we share, but before I can reach down and bring her to my lap, she shakes her head. "Don't deny me what is mine."

"Never." A quick tug to my trousers has me lifting my bottom, giving her just enough space to lower them down to my ankles. And she does, a small whimper escaping when my cock bounces free, slapping my stomach with the wet tip. *This woman is perfect. All mine.* "Do with me as you please."

"Thank you," she says with reverence and that surprises me, but I can't voice the question when her warm hand wraps around my shaft. "I've never done this before." The grip is tight, tighter than I expect, and my eyes roll back for a second before flashing red, the beast in me appreciative that I'm her first. Her only, and I growl, the sound of possessiveness—full of obsession.

I'm more turned on by that fact than anything I've experienced before.

That first downward stroke is slow, almost agonizing, but then she swipes a thumb over the tip and spreads the pearl-like bead. From underside to base, she rubs it in before exhaling against the taut skin.

Her mouth is so close. The scent of her arousal hangs heavy in the air, and knowing she's bare beneath my shirt, how easily I could take what I want, is punishment in and of itself. So cruel.

"You're going to be the death of the man many have tried—and all have failed—to kill, pretty girl." Tighter, her fist closes around my length and pumps me three times. On each upward turn, her mouth gets a little closer. "The end of me, and I'd never fight you."

"Or maybe I'm your rebirth." That small pink tongue slips from between her parted lips, just lightly grazing the slit. From head to toe, I feel as though struck by lightning as warmth spreads through my limbs. "Maybe I'm the reward you didn't expect, but I'm here and not going anywhere."

Before I can respond, though, she lifts a little to hover over my cock and then lowers her mouth, engulfing the head in warm, wet heat. Just a little past the tip is inside her mouth, and I feel as though she's taken every single inch down her throat. But then again, the sight is just as obscene.

Her lips are stretched, a little spit dribbling down the underside, and I can't help but to place a hand at the back of her head. Just hold it there as she swallows and takes in another two inches without pulling back, the hollowing of her cheeks creating the most delicious sensation, but then she toys with my entire existence.

Gabriella lifts until just the head touches her tongue, those expressive eyes on mine. "Guide me."

There's no curbing the need in me, the sounds leaving my chest loud and demanding, and I apply gentle pressure to her head. Inch by inch, Gabby takes me into her mouth until reaching the half where her hand still grips me; I pull her off.

Then again. I get her used to me and my thickness, how I force her mouth open, and then add another bit.

Her hand fists me, follows every upward bob and then down, before twisting up and then lowering until she relaxes further. She's new at this. All of it.

Sex is about enjoying yourself, not enduring, and when her unoccupied hand travels between her thighs, I know she's ready.

One thrust and those lips meet the base of my cock, kissing my now sensitive flesh. Another heady thing is discovering she has no gag reflex as she doesn't struggle, nor do her eyes tear up.

"You precious little thing," I coo, my fingers tightening on her hair as I pull her all the way off and force her to my level so I can kiss her. One harsh, yet quick swirl of my tongue across hers, tasting myself, before I push my pretty girl back to her knees. "Luckiest son of a bitch. Don't deserve such a treasure."

"You do deserve me." Gabriella doesn't wait and takes me back inside her mouth, bobbing her head a little faster, and I meet her with a thrust of my own. Damn, she feels good. Too good, and on the fourth drag of her tongue up the base before popping off, she winks at me. "I'm yours to cherish, Theo, but I also want you to use me."

"Say it again," I all but snarl, my balls heavy, pleasure licking at my spine. "Demand it."

"Use. Me." Her teeth nip at my flesh gently before removing her hand and cupping my sack. Just holds them, squeezes lightly, but that along with the quickened movement of her own hand between her thighs breaks me.

I fuck her face.

Hold her still, a hand on each side of her face as I thrust up and out, my movement almost too fast for her to match. Like this, I take what I want and the sudden cry from the back of her throat—the ripple of shivering—forces me closer to the edge.

One more pump, and I'm teetering.

On the next, I fall over, pulling her down until my cock flexes in her throat and spurt after spurt empties down the graceful throat of my mate. She doesn't make a face or pull back, swallowing all that I give her before licking me clean.

Gabriella blushes as she does the last part, her hand shaking a bit as I'm tucked back inside and I stare, a warmth spreading through me at how thoughtful she is. At this foreign feeling of being cared for.

Motherfucking precious.

"Did I do okay?" The timid quality of her voice doesn't sit well with me, and I stand up, gripping the back of her arms so she doesn't fall. I pull her into my arms, carry her in silence until we reach our private wing.

I'll have them bring her meal up here in a bit, but first...

Placing her on her feet, I take two steps back and motion with a hand to the door. "You are amazing and more than I deserve, but I'll prove myself worthy. Every minute—every second of the day—and I'll start now by worshipping that tiny pink cunt until you cry and beg, but even then, I won't stop. Your scent will be embedded into my flesh. Your pleasure is my greatest reward, pretty girl."

"Theo, I—"

"Go and present for your mate, sweetheart. I'm going to prove to you with my mouth how perfect you are in every way."

***

MUSIC PLAYS in the background a few nights later, the cacophony of instruments creating a melodic cadence that a group inside the room sways to in celebration of their king's mate. The pairs, many traveling from as far as America, twirl in a circular fashion while spectators talk quietly amongst themselves dressed in their best garments—sizing up their counterparts and how they can climb a little higher on the vampiric social ladder.

Greed. Lust. Hunger.

Each infiltrates the room as a hedonic edge of pleasure ripples through the air; my pretty girl watches this from her rightful seat at the center of it all. The choreography follows the light tone, the band keeping those celebrating appeased as those within the circle count steps and twirl, clapping at the end before bowing to their queen.

She's the main event.

The one they clamor to gain favor from after doubting her intentions.

Idiots. Not all of them, though. Tero and Marcia watch from the sidelines while Brodej and his wife each stand by a doorway. Then you have the elders who came forward and welcomed my soon-to-be wife—because I plan to tie myself to her in every fucking way—with open arms and a gentle demeanor and who keep away those attempting to move closer.

My girl is too smart for them, though.

Too cunning and unapologetic while seeing through each attempt. Her uninterested stare tells them as much.

My eyes cut to Veltross from my place behind a curtain, the drapery shadowing my face, but my subjects know I'm here. He's nursing his hand while speaking with a young blonde—his daughter—who's giving my mate her back, and the loss of an appendage, a wound to his ego, wasn't enough of a lesson it seems.

I smirk, knowing this won't be the last time I hurt him.

I'm going to enjoy it. Putting him and anyone who dare put a toe out of line in their place.

Those dancing switch partners then, their well-practiced hand maneuvers tapering into a more sophisticated waltz. They fall in line, and their forms, the aristocratic posture in their stance, become poised and full of finesse. Each step is refined, their pivots regal while onlookers give small applause that lasts no longer than three of Gabriella's heartbeats.

Silence follows. My pretty girl is riveted, yet nothing is more beautiful than her.

Simply sitting and breathing; two actions that on her I find captivating.

They do their best to ignore my presence, but hers they can't deny. She's dressed in an extravagant gown a deep shade of red reminiscent of the color of blood with a golden lace overlay. It's strapless, the bodice tight from her chest to knees where it then flares out a bit. The silk is soft, so feminine, but I do appreciate the lace that's provocative in its simplicity.

Gabriella stands out amongst the crowd; a modern to their more Victorian style, indicative of when most of these women were born.

Pretty girl's eyes traverse the room, her head held high and shoulders pulled slightly back. She's making eye contact with many, not shying away from the bright red eyes or the hungry black of those who still haven't been fed. If anything, I feel amusement through our bond, but no reproach or disgust while the humans in the room shiver in fear.

She's also tired. Her weariness is heavy.

"Not very nice of you, pretty girl," I say, my voice husky as her cherries and vanilla cream scent with a hint of arousal infiltrates my senses. More so when I drag a finger from her right shoulder to the left, my sharp nail leaves a minute scratch behind. No blood, just a slight pink. "You want me to paint the walls red before the others have eaten? Or kill my people."

"Well, you're no fun tonight." There's a pout on her lips, which pulls a chuckle from me. I've lost count of how many times I've laughed today alone. I'm a completely different man with her. "I thought indulging me was the highlight of your life. Besides, the auras of your dining choices are dark. So rancid. What hellhole did they crawl out of?"

"It is, and they are. Many come from the human jail or were caught misbehaving." Goose bumps rise across her skin where I skim my nails, then dip the tip of my fingers under the thin material of her dress over the ridges of her spine. Caressing her back, I enjoy the way she leans into me and the soft sigh that escapes those sweet berry lips. "But I'm a beast, sweetheart. A possessive one at that, and I don't want anyone to smell you—how wet you are for me."

"Can't help myself when you're close. Even if it's a few feet away."

Her confession makes me pause. It dawns on me. "You can sense me? How?"

Tipping her head back, Gabriella's eyes smile. Crinkle just the tiniest bit at the corner. "To me you are this force, an uncontrollable wave of pleasure that constantly licks at my flesh, pulling me in its direction. You are vibrant and strong, and the pulse never ebbs no matter how near or far you are."

Screams rend the air, and four male bodies fall to their knees, each one simultaneously cupping their necks while vampires hiss. Blood pours from a thin line, the scent creating a small frenzy that pulls the attention from my queen.

Many laugh. Others lick their lips.

She's not affected by any of it. Instead, her eyes remain on mine. The upward curve of her lips is directed solely for me. She really accepts me.

"Are you ready?" I ask a few seconds later, my face against hers, breath fanning her cheek.

"Ready for what?" Head tilting to the side, she shows me her neck. Tempting me.

"Motherfuck." It leaves me on a hiss, my cock hard and muscles contracting with the need—the urgency to get her somewhere private. I need her. All of her. And more so after this confession, a crumbling yet humbling truth that robs me momentarily of my senses.

The room disappears, and all I hear and see is her. I smell her sweetness and not the blood that drips to the floor when a body isn't fully drained.

My mouth waters and fangs descend; I pick my pretty girl up from her chair and cradle her small body to my chest, enjoying both the feel and the way her face turns into my neck, nuzzling me.

"Where are we going, King Astor?"

I shiver at her words. The hint of sass behind the formal address. "I want to show you something."

"Will I like it?"

"You'll fucking love it."

Gabriella

He walks us out of the room while the others begin to feed. The horrified screams of the humans still alive bother me, but not as much as I thought they would at first. Maybe it's because I'm attuned to nature and its course never changes with the times.

Life adapts, but instincts always remain the same.

To hunt and eat is ingrained in every species; it's how we survive.

Vampires drink blood.

Werewolves need meat—plenty of livestock and wild animals.

Fae like their sweet treats and creams.

My people lean toward a more vegetarian lifestyle, but depending on the coven, they do allow meat.

Humans have no preference and indulge in everything and anything. The good, the bad, and the illegal for the right price. They hunt more than they need, not understanding the delicate balance of life.

No species is above another.

There's always someone or something that poses a threat.

We are all connected one way or another in a large circle, a never-ending cycle of life that begins at birth and ends with death, while some like Theo enforce the balance.

It's something our parents taught us while young. Survival is never pretty or fair but collects just the same.

"Are you cold, pretty girl? Comfortable?"

"I won't deny that I'd love to change." Looking up, I give him a small pout. "The top is a bit constricting, and my breasts are used to being free. They don't need the support in this thing to be perky."

Amber eyes turn red, almost glowing as they lower to my chest. "You are perfect."

That's all he says before using a nail in the back to cut down the fabric encasing my upper body. The give is automatic, and I sigh in contentment, the digging sensation gone now.

"Thank you."

"Then thank me by never wearing something you are uncomfortable in." His lips press to my temple where he breathes me in, not once stopping his leisure pace back toward the animal sanctuary. Yet, instead of turning right where the large gate is, he veers left and then straight.

His pace picks up, and soon the sound of water reaches my ears. The soothing scent of a warm night wraps around me like a second blanket and my eyes close.

Gods, I needed this. Miss being outside.

Goose bumps rise on my skin, and I breathe in deep and then out, taking in the smell of grass and the sweet floral touch of sunflowers in the breeze. "This is more than nice."

Theo stops, his body lowering us both to the ground. "Open your eyes, beautiful."

"But I'm cozy."

"I want you to see this." His nails make quick work of removing every scrap of the dress from my body, leaving me bare for him. I'd refused any kind of undergarment; that was my compromise when the garments were delivered earlier by a nice girl named Marcia.

We didn't speak much; she kept her head down.

Yet, something about her called to me. Made me feel protective of her.

I'll have to ask Theodore about her later.

My eyes open at his low plea and I gasp, sitting up a little in his arms to get a better view of the area we are in. It's lush with foliage, all kinds of plants filling the vast open land that surrounds a lake with what looks to be a small waterfall. Then, there's the tree he's sitting against, the huge trunk growing strong and firm, taller than any other nearby.

Chest expanding, I take in another cleansing breath while he situates us a little better. With his legs spread, my back is to his front and that soothing purr is back within his chest. Its calming tone settles deep within my bones, and I find my eyes closing, my chest rhythmically following the rise and fall of his.

Not that he needs to breathe, and before I can ask him why the slow and even breaths, his lips trace from my temple to my cheek. The simple touch disarms any question I may have at the moment, and so does the way he removes his dress shirt and then drapes it over my front. "Rest, my beloved. I'll keep watch."

"I'm not tired."

"Our bond screams otherwise." A kiss on my jaw. "My apologies for not realizing you needed this sooner."

"Not your fault. I promise I'm—"

"No more arguing, pretty girl. Let me guard your sleep."

Exhaustion settles deep into my bones and my eyes grow heavy without my permission. Sleep creeps upon me; I feel heavy in his arms and don't notice when my hand reaches toward the earth and grabs a handful of dirt and grass, needing the feel of it between my fingers.

It's as if I'm drained and this is my way to recharge.

He cares. A low voice whispers, and I turn my face in its direction, following it.

I don't reach it, but Theo's kiss is the last thing my conscious mind remembers before all goes black.

"You have always been such a heavy sleeper, sister. Wakey, wakey." I recognize Isabella's voice, but I'm too annoyed by whatever is tickling my nose. It's obnoxious and after batting it away, the darn thing comes back more incessantly. *"Girl, can you please get up? We have so much to talk about."*

"Move that off my face or I will bite you," I warn, but that serves to make her laugh. The sound is just as loud as I remember, maybe even a little higher in pitch. *"Come on, Isa. Give me a few more minutes."*

"You'd risk our connection severing?"

Her words cause my brows to pucker. *"What are you talking about?"*

"Open your eyes." Brightness stings when I do and then something is angled in our direction, a covering to shield where we sit. Where are we? *"Same place you met Mom and Dad last time; this realm belongs to the family."*

"Theo." My voice is low, but she heard and smiles. I'm too busy looking around to ask her about the cheesy grin because I find nothing but trees and flowers surrounding us. The place is very similar to where my mate took me to rest. *"Where is he? I need to thank him then explain about—"*

"He's fine. See?" Her hand points in the direction past the large tree I remember from his land, but this time it's colorful, as if split by a rainbow down the center, and the thrumming within is the earth reading its surrounding auras. And just beyond that, in an area where darkness and brightness merge, the color a vibrant amber, I see him.

Theodore stands watch with his back to us, but his stance is clear: protect.

"Why am I here, Isa? Is everything okay?" Not that I look away

from my vampire to catch her expression, but the giggle that slips is unmistakably my sister. The fool is giddy. "Talk. Was your journey worth it?"

"Look at me and tell me what you see."

It's hard, but I pull my attention from Theo and look at Isabella. She's smiling, brighter and more at peace than I've seen her in a long time. There's also a bite mark on her neck. It's stark black and in the perfect shape of a wolf with warm eyes.

"You're fully mated." Not a question. The answer is sitting in front of me. "The alpha of alphas is your mate?"

"Yes and no." A fissure appears where her heart is, bright red, and I see it through the thin white gauzy dress she's wearing. "He hasn't accepted me yet."

"Did he reject—"

"No. Not fully."

"What does that mean?"

"That he tried, but I walked out before he could say the words." My lips open, nasty words on the tip of my tongue, but she shakes her head. "I've seen this happen, have relived the hurt in my vision many times, Gabby. It always ends this way. He's close to snapping, though, and the moment I leave his land, I'm his prized prey."

"I'm sorry." Closing the gap between us, I hug her tight. "You don't deserve this."

"We all have dark and rocky terrains to traverse. This is our path, and it will work out okay in the end, no matter the time it takes. That truth is what I'm clinging on to."

There's a bit of foreboding in that response, and I pull back with a raised brow. "So what's your next move then? Where are you?"

"We are going to meet back home in a week's time."

"We are?"

"Yes." Isa gets a faraway look, as if she's remembering something. "It's time to say goodbye to them properly and for our people, old and new, to come together. Your mate is strong and cares for you, as does mine, even if he is a bit stubborn, but together we'll defeat

what's to come. The Fae king isn't going to stand down easily, and Leo needs to be protected for more than one reason."

"Is he safe with Uncle?"

"For now, but I've already sent back word to bring him home."

"Okay. We will be there in a week." I'm suddenly jostled a bit, and Isa giggles. "The heck?"

"That man of yours is completely enamored with you, Gabby. He's one of the good ones."

"He is," I agree, looking toward the general direction I saw him last. Theo's no longer there, and I frown. "Even surrounded by darkness, embracing who he is born to be, there's a tiny light that sparks from within and sings to me. I'm whole when he's near."

"Then don't push him away or question the fates."

"Will you be doing the same?"

"Already am."

"How so?"

"Tough love on a wolf, an alpha wolf, is hard." Isa takes in a deep breath, shoulders squared, and then lets it out slowly. "By ignoring that strong and beautiful beast, I'm showing him what life will be like without me. Because once mates meet, there's no going back and the love between us will grow, morph into an obsession the more I remain out of his reach."

"But—"

"Wake up, Gabriella. The demon whose heart you hold can no longer remain patient."

My eyes snap open, and I'm back to the stunning piece of land Theo brought me to. I'm in his arms, nestled against his chest with my legs draped over his thigh. He moved me while I dream-walked, something my mother taught us to do when young in case we were ever separated, or worse, taken.

"You okay, pretty girl? You were mumbling in your sleep."

That man of yours is completely enamored with you, Gabby. He's one of the good ones.

"I am." Sitting up, I turn just enough to reach his mouth and place a kiss over his soft lips. He tastes of me with a hint of spice and I blush, remembering the days he spent teaching me with his hands and mouth how perfect for him I am. "But there are a few things I'd like to get off my chest before we move on."

"Go on."

We're still not close enough, and I move until I'm straddling his legs with the shirt carelessly tossed somewhere behind me. *Don't push him away or question the fates.* They put us together for a reason, and I'm happy with him. The way he watches me with unguarded passion and hunger makes me feel giddy, while my magic thrives under his darkness—almost seems to feed off it.

Theodore is death personified, and I was born to walk hand in hand with that power.

He's the physical manifestation of what I am—a sorceress blessed by a god to deal with his children. To take and give life.

"I came here with the intention to end whatever feud you had with my father, be it by death or truce." If he's surprised, Theo doesn't say anything, but his hand begins to run up and down my back in a soothing motion. Calming. "It wasn't a secret that you wanted me, and I was willing to play along if you let my people live in peace and under your protection. Your intentions weren't pure, Theodore, but neither were mine."

"What was your end game, pretty girl?"

"Your death at my hands and the freedom of my kind."

"Hmmm." That's all he gives me, his caresses never ceasing, though. *Must count for something, right?* Not that I have much time to ponder as he stands us up, holding me tight so I don't fall. My mate walks us to the edge of the lake and then inside the water, lowering me down so my feet touch the smooth rocks below.

"Please say something."

"I love you."

Gabriella

His words are my undoing.

They obliterate any doubt that he'd be pissed after my confession.

Instead, they fill me with warmth and my chest expands on a sob, the joy of hearing those three little words breaking me into a million pieces at his feet. Because I feel it too. This inexplicable desire to always be near and if he's happy—the desire to make him laugh and enjoy life with me is overwhelming. My soul cries out to him, my heart now unafraid because he truly won't reject us.

Theodore won't meet my eyes tomorrow and decide he doesn't want me.

"I could never reject you, love. Even if you did manage to kill me, my ghost would just haunt you like a lost puppy."

"Gods, I love you. I've been so scared that after hearing—" He cuts me off with his mouth, stealing my breath as his tongue slips between my eager lips. I'm kissing him just as hard, no soft touches or gentle sweeps when desperation burns from within and overtakes our senses.

I want him. All of him.

"Say it again, Gabriella. Tell me," my mate demands, his body vibrating as growls build in his chest. The vibrations rub my hard nipples against his pecs, his bare flesh and mine creating the most delicious friction.

"I love you, too."

"Fuck," he hisses, head thrown back as a loud snarl curls at his lips. The sound resonates throughout the land, animals scurrying to get away, but I bring his demon back under control when I lick the tip of his teeth. They're sharp and dangerous while the cool water laps at our feet, a complete contrast to how I feel inside.

I'm burning up. Hot and achy, and it's more than the other times he's touched me.

He's made me crave his touch. Every time we kiss or hold hands —the way he's always aware of my needs—is beyond sexy to me.

Then, my mind goes to the times his mouth and fingers have made me come, and I clench. My sex pulses in time with my heartbeat because I want more, too.

The mate bond is crazy and works fast, I won't deny it, but this surpasses what is normal.

I prickle with excitement when he's near me.

I want to make him happy.

I want to cut my heart out of my chest and present it on a silver platter because it solely beats for him.

Love is a wonderful thing like that. It's not selfish or self-serving; it grows and morphs, and always with the other person at the forefront. And seeing his smile—the one that is uniquely for me— widen and his eyes shine with wonder when I repeat the words back is the best moment of my life.

"This is my truth, Theodore Astor. I'm irrevocably yours." His mouth descends on mine again, just as hungry as before, while he reaches down and grabs a cheek in each hand, pulling me tighter against his body.

His pants can't hide the effect I have on him.

Moreover, their presence annoys me.

"Off," I moan out, rising onto the tips of my toes. "Get them off."

"We're going to finish our conversation, pretty girl." Theo's breathing hard, chest heaving as he tries to regain control of himself. I don't want him to. "You need to understand I'm not upset by what you said. If anything, I respect you all the more."

Gods, this man.

"Off."

"Gabriella—"

I cut him off, wrapping my fingers around him through the pathetic confines of his trousers. "This is what I want." The red of his eyes brighten, his fingers on my asscheek digging harder into my flesh while I feel him toe off his shoes. *I'll wear those bruises with pride.* "I'm giving myself to you without restrictions or rules; I love you. Make me yours."

"You're my treasure." Then he's walking us deeper into the water, not stopping until we're standing underneath the small waterfall. Surprisingly, the stream here is warmer than at the edge of this body of water. It's refreshing, feels good, but right now I want *all* of him, skin to skin, and nothing else registers.

My hands grip the back of his hair, tugging on the short strands at the nape and pull him down to me. It's my mouth that initiates this kiss, my tongue delving between his parted lips and caressing his.

I'm tasting his groans. Reveling in the near painful embrace, and yet it's not enough.

Circling my hips, I press my pussy against his shaft and slide up and down. My wetness coats us.

Another undulation and he brings two fingers lower, caressing my back entrance and adding pressure. Pleasure strikes down my spine, the simple touch not entering or moving, just adding a little force, and it shockingly sends a harsh tremor through my body.

"So responsive," Theo hisses before sliding to my pussy and rubbing the outside of my entrance. His fingers are wet with my juices and my sex pulses, a sharp cry leaving my lips. "Fuck, you're gorgeous when you come."

I can't respond. I'm lost to the sensation, yet craving more. So much more, and a pathetic whine leaves the back of my throat.

"Not enough."

"Are you sure?" My response to that is a bite to his lip, eyes narrowed. "So greedy, little girl."

"No holding back."

"Say it again." Theo's voice is deeper, and his eyes turn a darker red—hooded as he pulls us under the waterfall where a rock formation-like bench greets the back of my legs. The water's warmth still reaches us, misting, and it feels nice while creating a curtain of privacy. "Tell me what I need to hear."

"I love you, Theodore Astor." No hesitation from me.

"What you do to me." His body shivers, a harsh tremor that rocks me in his hold. "You're mine. Always mine."

"Yes. Yours." Mouth slanting over mine, he kisses me harder than before. Now he's all tongue and teeth and bites, giving me no chance to breathe as he explores every crevice before dragging his fangs down my chin and the column of my throat.

He stops at the vein there and licks a trail up to my ear. "One day you will wear my markings." A hard nip. "You'll become a vampire, crave what I do, and experience the raging lust that dominates my senses each time our eyes meet. You will beg me to change you, pretty girl, and I'll be honored to do so."

"But not today." Without me explaining, he knows. Understands, and more importantly, what I feel through our bond is pride.

"Not until your kingdom is safe."

"Thank you." Tears form in my eyes at that, but I don't let them fall. I'm focusing on us. On the way he makes me light up from within with a hunger so powerful I can hardly breathe. "You are everything to me, Theo."

"And you to me." Leaving a final kiss over the spot he wants to mark, his lips descend lower to my chest, flicking the tip of his tongue over my right nipple. Two quick licks and then I'm between his teeth—he's careful not to break the skin—and I'm arching to press closer.

At the same time, he pumps his hips against my core, sliding through my labia. The sensation is heavenly, a tease, but I do enjoy the sharp pain of his nail cutting me right above where his mouth is.

This wound is deeper than the other times, blood flowing, and he laps at it, drinking from me while torturing my tightened bud. Sucking, licking, and growling; he feeds from the wound while another wave of pleasure crests over me.

I'm sensitive. Each stroke of his tongue drives me higher and closer to another orgasm.

"Oh Gods," I moan out, loving the way he drags his blood-red lips from one nipple to the other. They're throbbing against his assault, so sensitive it's nearly painful. "Please, my King. I need to feel you inside."

"Fuck, sweetheart. You are sin incarnate." Another deep suck at the wound and I feel lightheaded, giddy from the affects. He doesn't take any more after that, but does let a string of his saliva fall straight into the wound and it tingles, the skin closing after a few seconds.

And I want to ask him about it, but then I'm leaning back on the stone with his mouth hovering over my sex.

Eyes on mine, he runs his tongue from slit to clit and back down again, slipping the tip inside my tight hole. It clenches violently, trying to pull his tongue in deeper, but Theo moves back. He hovers, breathing hard over my pussy before spitting on me.

The reaction is instant and I come, shouting his name as pleasure turns to tingles and then to hungry desire. Yearning. My core feels swollen, and I lift my hips in offering.

"More, please." I feel as though I've been struck by lightning. My pussy pulses.

"So beautiful when you beg in that tone." With the tip of a finger, he spreads his saliva and my wetness, mixing the two before pumping the same digit inside. It feels so good. "How desperate you are. How tightly you grip me."

"Inside…you…want," I mewl almost incoherently.

"My perfect, pretty girl. So pink and tender. So fucking small." Another rush of wetness escapes at his words. I'm shaking, clinging to the edge of the rock. He licks me again at the same torturous pace. "You're going to choke my cock, aren't you? Break my control."

"I-I'm ready for you." My hips rise to meet the next stroke of his finger, something that earns me a slap to the thigh. "N-no more waiting."

One blink, and he's above me with his heavy cock at my entrance. The tip rubs through my labia, spreading my lips apart again. Three times he does this before smacking my clit with it and I whimper, unable to do anything but take what he gives.

"Fuck," I grind out from between clenched teeth. My pointer finger slips on the rock's edge, and it stings, hurts, until pleasure unlike anything I've encountered before slams into me.

My eyes widen and my mouth drops open in a silent scream, body shaking beneath him. Every muscle in me spasms—a hard contraction that rips every part of my DNA and then makes it whole.

I feel as though I've been reborn.

The universe centers me and I meet his eyes, a mixture of red and amber now as he watches me. There's that purr I love in his chest, the melody soothing my soul while the rest of me embraces each thrust.

Because he rides me hard and fast. There's no time to anchor myself or meet him thrust for thrust.

Theodore Astor is claiming me. Every last inch.

"I want to be gentle with you." His forehead creases as he slams in again to the hilt. This time I do scream, the pleasurable ripple so profound that I can't do anything but cry out. "I want to worship and then lay the bloody world at your feet, but my desire for you overrides all common sense. I've never felt more like a demon than I do now."

"I love you." That's all I manage to say, my eyes rolling back as he picks up his pace. He's pounding me into the stone, and I don't care.

However, the minor cut on my finger deepens when he changes the angle of my hips the slightest bit. With my legs wrapped securely around his back, he lifts my ass off the flat stone, and it opens my wound.

Beads rise and fall, the scent catching his attention mid-thrust and then I'm whirled around as he sits and I'm straddling his thighs, taking him in deeper. My legs shake in this position, my walls pulsing against his girth, but then nothing matters as he takes my injured finger between his lips and sucks.

I feel the simple action down to my toes and lift, my instincts forcing me up until he's almost all the way out and then drop down. Hard and fast. It feels amazing, the pleasure so consuming, and I do it again and again, building a rhythm that I control while my mate watches through hooded eyes.

He lets me dominate the moment.

I know it's temporary, but the heady feeling makes me arch my back a little more. My hips pick up their pace until he adds a finger to my back entrance once again. To a place I never thought to be erotic.

The pressure of his finger is sublime, and I press back against it, earning myself a throaty chuckle. He still has my pointer in his mouth, a drop of my blood on his bottom lip. "I've discovered a new purpose for my life, Gabriella, and that's to bring you nothing but pleasure."

The force turns to a slight sting, but I'm wet from my earlier release and it's spread to my thighs and ass, making it easier for him to slip inside to the first knuckle.

"Theo!"

"That's right, pretty girl. Scream for me." With one hand on my hip and the other playing with my bottom, he bucks beneath me.

I find an anchor with a hand on his shoulder, fighting to stay upright, but I fail when he slips the rest inside and I feel so full. His cock and finger move inside me, impaling at the same pace—time—and I'm weeping, my tears falling onto his chest.

"My King," I whimper on the next hard thrust, body shaking. It hurts. It feels good. I'm all over the place, but when he releases my now healed digit from his mouth and I look up to meet his eyes, I shatter.

The love in them is my undoing.

"That's it, baby. See me and all that I am."

"I do," I moan as wave upon wave of pleasure batters my body like a tsunami. I'm limp in his arms, blissed out, but I can still make out the moment he comes.

The low, vibrating groan in my ear and the pulse of each rope of come as it coats my walls in him.

This will always be the most beautiful memory for me. The day my life truly began.

After a while, Theo nudges my face from his shoulder, silently asking me to look at him. "Are you okay?"

"Yes. Feel amazing." I move my hips a bit, testing to see if there's any discomfort and find none. "Is this because of you? What you did with your saliva?"

He nods, a smirk on his lips. "The healing qualities in my spit kept you from being in pain." Surprise colors my expression and I have so many questions on the tip of my tongue, but he simply taps the end of my nose while shaking his head. "I took your virginity, mate, but numbed the area where you bled and healed you while impaled deep. Your pussy will always be the perfect fit for my cock."

"That's both sweet and self-serving." I'm not mad, and the curl of my lips at the corner show him as much. "Very sneaky of you."

"I know." His playfulness wanes as he exhales roughly.

"Something wrong?' Nervousness comes in through our connection. The clarity in our bond is amazing, but knowing a little more of his origins and how he came to exist, it no longer surprises me. His strength—superiority—is unmatched by anyone I've encountered, and it makes sense that his relationship with his mate would be the same.

Special. Not the norm.

"Not wrong, but I do need to ask you a question." He's shifting his hand, as if nudging something. I'm tempted to look down, but the softness in his expression keeps me in place.

"You can ask me anything." Something cold slips onto my finger and my eyes widen, my chest growing tight. "Theo, what are—"

"Marry me." There's a knot in my throat, but my head bobs quickly in a yes. "Words, pretty girl."

"Yes. Goddess, yes."

Gabriella

I can't stop admiring my ring, loving the way the large ruby stone glints off the sun coming in through the treetops. *So pretty. The same shade as his eyes when aroused.* But then again, since he proposed I've been living in a constant *la la land* loop where nothing but him exists.

"You really want to get married? Is that something important to your people?" I ask from my back, floating a few feet from the waterfall. I'm not looking at him, but his stare is intense over my bare-to-the-night body.

"Not really." Voice rough. Breathing labored. "The moment bites are exchanged, it is the equivalent of."

My brows furrow. "So is our bond not complete?"

"Nothing has ever been as strong." Theo steps in beside me, his hand gliding up my thigh until reaching my core. He cups me, and I spread my legs a little wider. I'm already slick, so ready for the next round. "You are a powerful sorceress, while I'm the son of a god—

our bond was sealed the day you took your first breath, pretty girl. We are unstoppable."

"Is that why I can sense your emotions? Even without the traditional mating?"

"It is." With the tip of two fingers, he spreads my wetness before sinking both in deep. I cry out while he pumps them in and out, his hardness brushing against my leg. "You and me, we're a forever kind of madness. We will give and take. Destroy and build. But more importantly, we will always be one heart, mind, and soul."

"I love you, Theo." His fingers leave me, the blur of his body moving to stand between my parted thighs. I'm gently pushed into a semi-upright position, right over his hard cock, and with his eyes on mine, he sinks in. "Gods."

"We are one."

My cheeks heat up at the memory, and I squirm a bit.

"You okay, Gabriella?" That timbre of his, the velvety quality does things to me, and I bite back a moan. "Need something?"

"I'm fine." There are people behind us, a solid formation where his guards and a few curious helpers ride while trying their best to keep to the shade. Vampires don't normally expose themselves during the day, preferring the darkness to conceal their bodies, but today was inevitable.

There's a cloaking spell my father used often when traveling through unclaimed territories that made him undetectable to both people and nature. Unseen and with no trace, he could walk over a pile of fall leaves and you'd never know. There would be no sound. No scent.

This is the land where all species, exiles of their communities, live freely and without laws. These aren't the nicest people, most are rabid or have crimes against their coven or pack to attest for, but they're keen predators. Always alert.

And it's this incantation, one with a deviation added to tweak and fit any scenario, that's kept the vampires with us protected from the harsh rays that would normally hurt them. Like an invisible umbrella above them, following us as we go.

"Do you need us to stop so you can rest?" Theo's warm breath tickles my ear while his arm around my waist tightens. "Are you hungry?"

"No need. We are almost there; I sense them."

I'm heading back to the place I called home until recently. The Moore's property line isn't far from where we are, and I can feel the protection spell already reaching out and recognizing me.

We've been riding for quite some time now; the members of his coven are covered from head to toe to avoid the sun, while Theo rides in just an undershirt behind me on a grumpy horse.

The vampires are uncomfortable with the feeling but don't question me. Instead, they follow through the woods while a huffing neigh greets my ears…again.

We're riding through familiar terrain and almost back on my family's property. I'm elated, can't wait to see everyone, while my horse gives me a bit of a cold shoulder.

I'd forgotten about Onyx, my attention overtaken by my mate, yet Theodore stepped in and found him. Theo took care of our family's horse personally without my knowledge, feeding and grooming him for the last two weeks.

"I'm sorry." I lean forward a bit to better reach the area between his ears and scratch. "I'll make it up to you with an extra bucket of apples. Just don't be grumpy." His ears twitch; he heard and understood the word *apple* very well. They're his favorite treat. "Forgive me?"

"Are you seriously trying to win the horse over with food?"

"It's called a bribe…" looking at him from over my shoulder, I mock-glare "…and yes." No shame. And I might be a bit sulky that Onyx seems to like him more than me. "This is all your fault."

"My fault?"

"You're lovable." A blunt statement, and one he laughs at too, our horse matching his laughter with a snort. "So fix this."

"Have I told you I like you a little petulant, sweetheart? Be a brat for me, and I'll reward your ass later."

"Gods, you can't say things like that. Not now."

"Who's going to stop me?" Then he licks the area his bite will go, and goose bumps rise on my skin. From head to toe, I feel the flat of his tongue, the gentle flick with the tip that settles in my core. As if his mouth was on me there.

"Me." Weak. No real strength behind it.

"Liar."

He doesn't get to respond, though. We break through the trees and there are thirty guards standing just inside the perimeter blocking us from passing—until they see me.

Before I can speak, they're on their knees and my sister is rushing through the center, coming straight for me.

I hear her say my name, but before my smile can spread, snarls and growls overthrow all sound.

There's a large wolf rushing for my sister, sliding out in front of her and my mate does the same, jumping high above Onyx and me and landing in a protective stance between us.

Our vampires do the same.

So do the wolves.

They stare each other down, both in a fighting stance before Isa and I realize what's happening.

"What's your business here, leech?" a large, naked man asks. His voice is loud, booming through the field while ignoring a very pissed-off Isabella. "How dare you step into—"

"Who the hell are you to question me, mutt?" The vampires all bare their teeth, their nails growing longer than I've seen thus far, but it's the anger contorting Theo's face that makes me react. "Stand down and in your lane, Xadiel. Don't tempt me."

"Make me, you—"

"Enough!" Isa and I say in unison, and the members of our army present finally come to their senses. Augusto reaches us first, taking his place one step in front of us much like the others attempt to do, but I hold a hand face down to the ground and they move aside, letting us reach my mate and who I assume is hers.

The vampires and wolves watch us, but it's the two men almost nose to nose that seem to not get the memo.

"Theodore, please come here," I say, voice low, but he ignores it with a shake of his head. Instead, he says something too low for anyone else to hear, and judging by Xadiel's response, it's offensive.

So much so that the latter half-shifts and snaps his teeth at my mate. Stupid move.

"Isa…?"

"Do it."

Not waiting another second, and right as Theo's hand wraps around Xadiel's neck, I call upon their souls.

"*Prohibere*." My love might think he doesn't have one, but he does. He's just as large, dominating, and imposing, but bends for me when called forth like all the others do. Werewolf and vampire; shock sets in as they stop. No movement or sound, and Isa rushes to her mate as I do mine. "*Satus*."

"The fuck was that?" Xadiel asks, but my eyes are on Theo's, hoping he isn't mad at me. "Isa, did you do that?"

"No, but my sister did."

"You are so amazing, pretty girl." A whooshing breath escapes my chest at his response, a giggle bursting through. "And no, not mad. Although, the mutt does need to learn some manners."

"Name the time and place."

"For the love of!" Isa trails off, but the half-scream, half-groan she makes has her mate dropping the attitude. "I told you my sister was coming with her mate."

"You never said he was a—"

"Quit the insults already. Both of you." My tone leaves no room for argument, and Theo is the first to extend a hand and I'm proud of him. "Thank you, love."

"Happy wife. Happy life." The wink he sends my way causes me to flush, but it's nothing compared to my sister's squeal a second before she engulfs me in a hug. It's tight and she's loud, but the tension drops a bit when she sees the ring.

How can it not when they all stare at it?

As if they know something I don't.

"What?" I ask, my eyes ping-ponging back and forth. "What's wrong?"

"He gave you the bloodstone of Thanatos." *God of death. Part of the underworld and my keeper.* "The stories are true, then? How else would you have such power?" Xadiel isn't accusing nor is there hostility in his tone—more like understanding.

"Theodore?" I'm shaky. Not understanding, and yet...

My father took a break and a human girl as his.

You can't kill what's never truly been alive.

You've been mine since your first breath.

"He is my father."

"You're a half?"

"I am." His eyes go from amber to red, looking at every single person present. "Speak of this to anyone, even if it's your kin, and I will kill you and them. Only the most trusted vampires in my coven know this. Understood?"

"Yes."

"Good." Grabbing my hand, he lifts it to his lips and kisses the finger with the large engagement ring. "You have always been my destiny; I understand that now. I was wrong to ever think a mate was a curse when you are the reason I'm alive."

WHAT HAPPENED OUTSIDE EARLIER today has been left alone for the time being, as if it never happened, and the focus quickly turned to my parents. Their spirits have been calling out to me all day, a bit nervous, but I put it down to our saying goodbye.

It's as hard for them as it is for us. All three children will be in attendance, and there are strangers on their land that, for the time being, pledge loyalty to the Moore family.

Isa and I left the men to their own devices shortly after Theodore's threat, leaving them to handle whatever they need to discuss as the early afternoon sky turns to twilight. The chants of our people have been filling the day with songs of hope and peace—for the rest of their eternal souls.

They've gone all out as has been instructed, every coven member dressed in their finest white while the children wear black, a symbol of our mourning. Of how deeply their departure has cut, but more than that, I'm grateful for the man now standing beside me in a crisp suit, always so handsome, as my uncle and his wife walk through the door to our home fifteen minutes before we are due to begin.

I still haven't forgotten our last conversation. How he refused to help us.

"Gabriella," Uncle Roberto greets, but doesn't come close as Theo shoots him a dirty look. "I'm happy to see you, my child. Happy to know you and your sister are on the right path."

His response makes me bristle. "Evening, Uncle. Zia."

"We need to talk after, my niece. Please, I have so much to explain."

"Why now?" Theo wraps an arm around my side and tugs me close, an action my father's brother doesn't miss. "You abandoned us."

"I promised your father not to interfere."

Before I can demand more, a lanky figure comes flying at me, almost knocking me back. Theo rights us. "Gabby!"

"Leo!" I respond with just as much enthusiasm. I'm so happy to see him. Pulling back, I inspect him for bruises or cuts…loss of weight, and I'm satisfied to see he's well. That the lost and haunted look from before is nearly gone and he's found rest. "How have you been, your majesty?"

"Ughh, I forgot how annoying you guys are. Get out of my kingdom."

"No can do, squirt. By blood and pact," Isa begins, bumping his shoulder with one of hers, brow raised.

"We are one," both Leo and I finish, and the others in the group smile.

"Good." Isabella looks over at her mate, the man so tall and muscular, easily taking most of the space in the small entrance we are in. Most of our guests are each in their own group, standing off to the side and warily watching the others. *That won't do.* "Now, love."

A sharp whistle rends the air and at once, all turn to look in our direction. His men, though, bear their necks and wait for further instruction.

"We are about to begin." Those of Wiccan descent walk out. They're heading to the newly made living tribute on the territory to wait for us. "Vampire and werewolves, I ask that you remain silent throughout and respect our traditions."

Their leaders glare.

They fall into two separate lines and walk out through opposite exits.

With them out, I turn to our mates still here. "If you two decide not to come with us, we understand and won't be upset."

"We're going."

"Pretty girl, try and get rid of me."

Gabriella

andles light the path to the family mausoleum.

The light shines bright with a swaying flame, and the closer we get, the higher they burn. Then there's the sudden growth of Parma violets all along the outside, the flower giving off a hint of a lavender fragrance that reminds me of Mom's favorite oils, something she'd burn every night to calm the house and spirits always surrounding the home because of me.

They endured so much because of me. Because of Isa.

We didn't ask to be born with gifts.

We didn't ask to be desired by many.

"I miss them, too." My face turns to Isa's, and the tears in her eyes make my own water. We've always been in sync with each other's emotions, that twin thing, but when it mirrors the other's like today, it magnifies and squeezes heart muscles. "But one day, we will be reunited once again. They'll be there at the end of our journey to welcome us home."

"One day." With my hand in each of my siblings', I walk us

forward and inside the resting place where our parents will remain for all time. While we believe in eco-friendly burials, my family does hold a bit of non-traditional customs, the large mausoleum on the property being one of them. This space is private and only those of the Moore last name may enter, but more importantly, it keeps a piece of their essence for the family to privately conjure or simply spend time with.

The moment we step inside, there's movement around us, a swirling of air inside an enclosed space and it sweeps over our joined hands, blessing the strength we all share. I can smell Mom's sweet floral scent and Dad's patchouli. I can feel a hug, binding all five of us before the presence disappears out of the door.

It's time.

The plaque on the wall that holds both urns and the small, lavender-infused satchels with a small amount of ash is open, the stone covering on the floor...

"Who opened it?"

"That would be your mate. He wanted to make sure you didn't lift a finger." Leo's tone holds amusement while my face registers shock. "And before you ask, that man is above magic. Nothing seems to affect him."

"Okay." Because what else can I say? I've always known him to be strong, unmovable, but this surprises me.

Maybe it's because of who he is. What he is.

Maybe it's because I've witnessed his iron will.

Or maybe it's because he allowed me to...

He allowed me to bend his will. That sneaky devil.

"Let's begin." Isa follows the chant that so many outside are already singing, their voices reaching a high crescendo when we remove the closed burial vase. They chant a wish for those who've passed, their former king and queen, a happy afterlife and prosperity for those who remain in their shoes.

Leo carries the urn, and I light the incense. *"Te amo. Invenire in pace."*

"Invenire in pace," my brother repeats before walking out behind Isa.

I take an extra moment after they leave to place a kiss on the cold stone; the pain of loss has been replaced by Theo's affection, but I would've loved for them to share in this moment of happiness with me. To walk me down the aisle and then see me round with a baby in the future.

"You were right. He's amazing, and I hope we make you proud."

THE CEREMONY BEGINS the second we enter the ground where we will spread their ashes. We chose not to go the traditional Wiccan route, not when it would be left to their children to speak and conduct—not when we are hit with the reality of their death once again.

They say you never get over the loss of a loved one, and it's true.
Some days the pain lessens, and you remember the good times:
Family dinners.
The laughs.
The closeness we all shared.
On others, we're left with the painful reminder that someone's greed destroyed our family.

Today is one of those sad days. Tears flow down our cheeks while those around us sing my mother's favorite song, the one she danced to at her wedding to our father. Then they move onto an old classic rock song from the human world that he would hum when strolling across the territory, checking perimeters or simply helping someone in need.

The two say more than we ever could. More than an anecdote from a friend or fellow coven member.
Love. Family. Peace.
Those three were their symbols, and we honor them by letting go and looking toward the future.

Looking back, I meet Theo's eyes and find so much love in them. He's everything my parents told me he'd be in that dream after we first met. The key that brings us together.

Because of him, I'm not alone and my people will thrive once more.

Because of him, we are back home, forcing Xadiel to come after Isa and show his true feelings. He'll mark her soon enough, make her happy, but also be there for her people.

And together, we'll all be here for Leo to grow into the wizard king I know he is.

I will one day see you again.

When the singing comes to an end, my siblings and I approach a hole in the ground with a plant beside it. Nature is a large part of our beliefs and way of life, and there is no better place to rest than to become one with what you cherish.

Our parents will rest here.

They will fertilize the ground where a large willow tree will grow, providing shade and a resting place for our coven members for generations to come. Kneeling on the ground, I find their tethers to this world, my fingers digging into the dirt, and slowly send them on their way. "*Vale.*"

No sooner has the word left my lips that the ever-present essence that's been following me for months is gone. It hurts, but it's the right thing to do, and my siblings join me on the ground.

Leo pours their combined ashes while Isa brings in the plant that will one day be large and beautiful, while I press in the dirt all around the base. We each pat it, making sure it stands firm, and then rise to face those attending.

Many faces hold tears, their emotions a mixture of grief and pride.

We will be okay.

And I truly believe that.

THE NEXT DAY is a little bit livelier. Everyone's outside catching up when a familiar face waves me over. She's standing next to Christopher, the last remaining Rossi, and a still-out-of-place Marcia. The younger female seems so lost, lonely, and I've vowed to bring her along as much as possible. She's missing the guidance of a mother, and while I can't fill those shoes, a sister is something I can offer. "I'll be right back."

"Everything okay?" Theo asks, his eyes shifting to the woman standing not far from us. "You know her?"

"I do. She's a survivor of the Salicio Coven."

"Survivor? I didn't end them."

"But someone made it seem as if you had." An idea occurs to me then, and I grab his hand, tugging him with me. "Come. I feel as though we are missing something important here."

Meera eyes Theodore as we come closer, fear and respect on her face. She also curtsies, which I find awkward and so antiquated. "Your majesties."

"Please don't. Not to me, Meera."

"I'm sorry, but old habits are hard to break."

"How so?" Theo asks, his arm over my shoulder while not so subtly tucking me into his side. Always touching me.

"My father would beat any woman that didn't do so for the males in our coven. It was just another way to break us, make us submissive." *I wish he were alive just so I could kill him myself.* "From children to the old, he didn't care much for the females of his tribe. We were worth no more than the blood in our veins and to produce more males. It's why he killed the two children he adopted. Neither fit into his sick world."

"What about the children we found in the hidden cavern? There were boys—"

"He found those to be defective. Weak."

"Who killed him?"

A small tremor runs through Meera, fear flashing in her eyes, but I'm proud of the way she squares her shoulders back and breathes out her tension. It might take her a minute, but a sudden calmness fills her with enough strength to meet our eyes once again. "My father was feuding with the fae king for more territory, unhappy with the three-way agreement between the Salicios, Rossis, and Marianos. The latter killed him with the help of the fae and traitors from your lands. They needed to make it seem as if it were vampires."

Where is the Mariano widow and child? I thought they'd be here?

"How are you alive? How do you know it's someone from my coven?"

"The cell I was kept inside of was deep beneath the ground, but everyone inside could still hear the outside world and many conversations were held there. It was part of the torture." Meera exhales roughly and her hands shake, but Marcia takes one of them in hers for support. I appreciate that. I'm proud of her for stepping out of her shell a bit. "Help was so close, many times standing against the damn tree hiding the truth, but our pleas were never heard until…"

"Until what?"

"Only a powerful witch can sense that level of dark magic and break through its bind. Isa and Gabby are the reason so many are alive today; I owe her my life and…"

Another being steps into the clearing and in his hands are two males, both beaten and bleeding, but more important is the way he's watching Meera.

Tero drops the two bodies and slowly walks over, his warm pastel eyes filling with so much gratitude and love. He's at Meera's side in an instant and down on one knee, his head bowed in a submissive pose while his sister gasps. Marcia's warm eyes, the color of her animal, become wet with tears and she smiles at me.

A real genuine one that lights up her face. *They're connected.*

I hear the voice in my mind and tilt my head, eyes widening as rationality merges with awe. Marcia spoke to me telepathically. She trusts me enough to do so. *They are.* I'm hoping she hears that and a second later she claps, catching the attention of Theo.

He doesn't ask what's happening, but I have a feeling he knows, and our bond is happy.

"Mate."

"Mate." Meera and Tero whisper in unison, bringing our attention back to them. She pulls him up and into an embrace, nodding in silent acceptance.

Guess I don't need to ask her to come be my assistant back on Theo's territory.

"I'd be happy to help as well," Marcia's voice comes through, so timid and shy. She's a few years younger than me, not by much, but still needs guidance. "If you'd like. In between training, that is. Tero would kill me if I abandon that."

"Then we have a deal."

"Yeah?" She smiles a little bigger, the charming scales of her cobra flashing in appreciation. "For real?"

"Yes. You learn to shift while I practice a few spells."

"Like an accountability partner?"

"Exactly like one."

Vampire King THEODORE ASTOR

"State your name and business for being on the Moore property," Tero asks, circling around the bound man. We're back home and in my prison, my guests all standing beside me as a half-shifted python interrogates the asshole.

Both men were a part of King Larue's army, their clothing indicating that they're assassins for the fae crown. One is alive, the other no longer breathing.

"I don't answer to…*fuck*!" The man to the left curses, spitting out two knocked-out teeth from Tero's fist, the scales on his hand now covered in the blue blood that indicates their species.

"Last chance to play nice and answer; my boss doesn't appreciate disrespect."

"Fuck you and your boss. Our king is the one true ruler of all."

"Is that so?" I step into the only source of light in the room, a beam of sunlight that comes from a tiny window with a very specific view. There's a tree there, tall and leafless with a single corpse hanging from the tallest branch—his companion. He's already shared so much. Had no real backbone once introduced to the kind of pain I can produce. "Please, do tell me more about this one true king."

"I won't. You might as well kill me now."

"Or maybe I can share a story with you while my friend here teaches you about pain." Turning to Xadiel, I point to the large bucket near his feet. It's empty now, but history has proven time and time again that those under high duress can't control their bodily functions. The werewolf does so without pause, his understanding and mine tenuous, yet works. What matters are the sisters and keeping them happy. The need of a mate will always come first, even if in private we'll come to blows eventually. "Thank you."

"Always glad to help." The deep timbre of his voice resonates throughout the small cement room, and my guest shakes in fear. *Interesting.*

"Let us begin." Tero fully shifts then; his large reptile form half coils on the ground while the upper sits high enough to stare the idiot in the face. Eye to eye. "Your name is Henri, age twenty-eight, and you're a high-ranking member of Larue's guard. His puppet."

"I'm not...*merde*!" His shout of pain brings a smile to my face. Tero lands the first bite to his thigh, digging his teeth in deep before yanking back. A chunk lands on the ground, the cold splat and flowing blood causing the vampires inside the room to hiss. Brodej controls himself, but his wife isn't as merciful and her bloodlust is quite a thing to see.

She's worse than he is.

"Try again." I nod at Tero, who strikes the opposite leg. "Am I right or wrong."

"Right." He didn't last long at all.

"Okay. Moving along." The python doesn't tear the flesh this time, but simply leaves the torn piece hanging from his thigh still attached. "Larue sent you to spy on the Moore children. He's looking for something your friend wasn't aware of; the poor man didn't have much upstairs."

"Yes."

"What is he looking for?"

"I can't tell you, he grits out, the pain settling in deep. "Can't betray my kind."

"They betrayed you with this bullshit assignment. Or was there more to it?" When he doesn't respond, Tero embeds his teeth deep into the fae's side, right over his ribs, and gnaws back and forth until a second piece lands beside the first. The jagged edge of the cut is ugly, and from the looks of it, won't heal right either. "Don't worry, you're here to corroborate what the crowned prince and your dead friend already told me. Both of them were quite chatty after a few well-placed cuts."

"Just end me."

I won't kill him. He'll go back to Larue with a personal message from me.

You don't come for what is mine.

Gabriella is my mate, and her family will always have my loyalty and protection.

"Who were you there to kill, Henri?"

"Please stop." Another attack, this time to his shoulder. "It wasn't Gabriella he wanted to take."

A deep rumble builds in Xadiel's chest, and Henri notices his mistake.

"Who were you planning to put your filthy hands on?" Xadiel's half-shifted form steps into the light, and Tero moves back after I nod. The werewolf has the right to defend his mate. *He's family now.* "Speak, you pathetic cunt."

"We weren't going to hurt her."

"You were coming for my mate?"

"Just to draw out the other. My king is looking for two artifacts he believes are the source of the twins' true magic."

"Why?" Xadiel's claws extend as he grips the man's neck, breaking the skin. Henri cries out, his body bowing, fighting to move away, but even without the chains, he couldn't. The werewolf alpha is poised to end him. "What does he want with it? Them?"

"The subjugation of your species."

"And?" I ask, then place a hand on Xadiel's arm. "Follow the plan. He'll be useful."

"Doesn't mean I can't hurt him."

"Not at all." Stepping back, I grit my teeth and wait for the confirmation of my suspicions.

"Answer him, fae scum. What are his plans?"

"To sacrifice them to Ares with the use of the Stygian blade. He wants his protection during the inevitable war—offering their blood in exchange for an allegiance and the gift of the hidden artifact."

"Thank you." My eyes meet Xadiel's right before I walk out of the room. He can do anything he pleases *but* kill him. He'll go back to Larue with a gift from me. The royal I'm keeping a few cells from Henri watches me leave with so much hate while nursing the hole where there once was a finger and ring.

He can blame his father for his predicament.

They'll learn a valuable lesson soon enough.

Gabriella is sacred. Untouchable.

And I'll be more than happy to prove this to Larue before I slit his throat.

THERE'S a group of vampires waiting on me the moment I step out of my dungeons later that night. They're faces hold contempt, while the leader, a mediocre fighter at best, eyes me with disgust.

I'm going to enjoy this.

"Speak."

One word, and those with him take a step back. Hands shake.

"You've betrayed your kind by laying with a witch." Strike one. "You've lost sight of what matters to your people, who our enemies are." Strike two. "We do not mingle with mutts and easy bitch—"

"Strike three." My fangs descend, eyes narrowed at the man who dares insult me and mine. "State your claim like a man, and don't waste my time. I have wedding preparations to get back to."

That incenses him, his own teeth dropping. "That wedding will never come to be. We'll kill…"

"I'm sorry, I didn't catch the rest of that?" My hand snaps to his neck, hold tight, and the pressure causes the bones in his jaw to crack. The sound is loud, and every vampire nearby pauses what they're doing as I hold him by the neck with his feet off the ground. "You were denying me something? You have something to say against your queen?"

"A witch will never be my queen."

"Who's going to stop me?" No one steps forward. His friends have lost their bravado, especially when Tero and Xadiel come out of the building wearing the blood of a traitor. "Go on. Speak up."

"I will."

"Is this a formal challenge?"

"Yes." Garbled, but I'll take it. He'll heal before the fight.

"So be it. You have an hour to prepare and meet me on the training grounds outside the castle."

"THEO, what the hell is going on?" Gabriella rushes onto the training grounds. The women with her are close behind and all wear the same expression: worry. "Why are you fighting for the crown?"

"Are you scared I'll lose?" Right thing to say as she glares, those green orbs shooting fire my way before her hand smacks my shoulder. "Is that a yes?"

"Heck, no. I pity who rose against us." I love that. She sees my problems as hers. We're a unit. "Where is the idiot?"

"Walking toward us."

"Him?" Her laugh rings out, catching those around us by surprise. They don't expect her to outright mock my challenger, but appreciate that she does, and this wins her the respect of many who've been on the fence. They'd never outright say it, but vampires don't mix well with other species, and my taking a sorceress for a mate is provocative. Challenges the status quo. "Please tell me you are joking?"

"I'm not, pretty girl. He's upset over the recent changes." *Mainly her. What she represents.*

"You mean me. No reason to sugarcoat."

"Yes."

"Funny." The disdain in her inflection is clear. She sees him as beneath her. "That coming from someone I could end without moving more than my hand."

"I'd pay you in gold to see that."

"I'd do it for free." Fuck, the mouth on her...

My cock jerks at the memory of her on her knees with my full length down her throat. The way she swallowed for me, cleaned me until there wasn't a single drop of my release left.

"So fierce, my mate. How'd I get so lucky?"

"You mean cursed to have that as—"

"Make it quick, my love. We have an afternoon full of wedding preparations to complete before having dinner with my sister and *Alpha Xadiel*." The little brat's emphasis on her brother-in-law's name isn't lost on me. My opponent tries to snarl at her, his lip curling, but reins it in with one look from me. "Really? You back down that fast and still believe you can win?"

"I don't answer to you."

"Then deal with him." Standing on the tip of her toes, Gabby nips my bottom lip and pulls back, raking her teeth across it. "By the way, do you like the idea of white or black for my wedding dress? Isa and Meera keep asking, and it's driving me insane. I'm fine either way, but would prefer it if you choose."

"Black. All black with a hint of red somewhere of your choosing."

"Thank you!" Looking at the other vampire, she snorts. "You're an idiot."

My mate walks away, and I track her movements until she's standing with her group again. Her smile is saucy, while the other women wear varying degrees of emotions across their faces—from annoyed to insulted and finally angry. Marcia is much like her brother, loyal and protective, even if the younger shifter has yet to master her abilities.

So far, she does well with Meera and Gabriella, clinging to them as no other woman here will talk to her. They're scared of what she and her brother can do, but more so her, since the bite of a cobra is quite painful even for a vampire.

She can't kill them, but her poison is potent enough to knock Brodej on his ass.

We know this from their first encounter.

He and his wife learned to respect them the hard way.

Xadiel steps between me and my opponent, holding a hand up. All noises cease. "This is a fight for the crown. No winner will be declared until one of the two is dead and the victor holds up their detached head."

"Rules?" the other guy asks. I never cared enough to ask him for a name.

"None. Begin." Before Xadiel steps out of the circular pit, I have an untrained and very disappointing vampire rushing toward me with his nails extended. He goes for my face, but misses and as he stumbles past, I kick him in the back. This sends him crashing a few feet away, his face landing on the stone bench near a water fountain. It cracks, as does his cheek.

I stand and wait for him to compose himself. I'm in no rush.

"You're weak." He spits on the ground; a tooth having been knocked loose lays there. "A pathetic excuse for a king."

From the corner of my eye, I see Veltross enter the grounds and make his way toward my mate. There's nothing in his hand, his sword and armor not on, but I still don't like him close to her.

A punch lands on my jaw, but I don't so much as turn my head.

Then another, and still the same response. He has no strength behind his hits. Uncoordinated and untrained.

Veltross says something that makes Gabriella and her sister glare, their body language radiating anger, but I don't move toward them as my mate brings a hand to his face and with a low utterance, brings the general pain. It registers in his expression before he places his one hand over his chest, a show of fidelity that I can tell is fake.

No. He's not offering his loyalty but pissing her off instead.

I catch his next punch and then wrench the fist clean off from the wrist, tossing it aside. Next is his arm, the left and then right, leaving him without a way to hit.

He's too stupid to use his feet or body.

"You asshole!" the man screams; his pain is a beautiful thing. "Fight me like a man."

"I am." Landing a direct strike to his mouth, I take out the remaining front teeth and dislocate his jaw. The next one breaks his nose, and the last is hard enough to damage the right eye. It bursts from the impact, the fluid inside running down his cheek as tears would.

Yet, I'm not done.

His limp body falls to the ground in pain, and I straddle his chest, not allowing him to curl up into himself. He was never a challenge for me. Not even a distraction.

My pretty girl is handling herself just fine and is walking away from a still-shocked Veltross.

Xadiel and Tero are heading their way.

Brodej is kissing his mate goodbye, leaving on a special assignment.

"My mate was correct to call your arrogance idiotic. You were never a match for me."

"Please don't. I was hired by—"

"I know, and they shall pay." With one hand around his throat, I squeeze until it collapses under the pressure. Not that it takes much

—he truly was an idiot—and after a tug, I raise the horrified head up for my enemies to see.

They have a spy. So be it.

Scum always rises to the surface.

Before I can fully stand, though, I have a sweet little body wrapped around me and the head falls, thumping against the ground while a berry-sweet pair of lips press against my own. She's pliant in my hold and squirming to get closer, but it's the pride in her eyes that makes me hard as fuck.

So much love. So pure.

"Congratulations, my King."

"Thank you, my soon-to-be wife."

Vampire King
THEODORE
ASTOR

Gabriella is walking toward me in a simple, long silk dress that accentuates her every sinful curve. In her hands is a bouquet of bright red roses, their color a stark contrast to the black of her garment.

Simply stunning.

The traditional wedding march plays; Meera is behind the keys while our guest sit, eyes riveted on the beauty almost to the altar where I stand with an oracle. She's from Gabby's coven, the woman who replaced her dead grandmother and whose eyes shine with pride at my pretty girl.

The song comes to an end as her small hand lays over mine, letting me guide her up the two steps. A hush overtakes the crowd, a soft breeze swirls around us, and my mate smiles, eyes misting, yet no tears fall.

She's not sad. The bond thrums with happiness and excitement.

I'm a lucky motherfucker.

Pay attention, she mouths, rolling her eyes when I ignore the chastisement. I just can't look away from her face when the oracle begins, nor when she speaks about the sanctity of marriage or the importance of communication.

I hear it all. Every word.

Yet nothing can pull me away from the peace and pleasure my mate feels.

It mirrors my own.

"The ring, King Astor?" Patting my chest pocket, I grab it and without prompt, slip the band that matches her engagement ring onto Gabriella's finger—the place it will stay for eternity.

"You may carry on," I say, voice thick from my own sentiments.

"Okay." The old woman chuckles a bit and my wife's lips twitch, amused by my actions. "Your ring, Gabriella?"

"I have them." The gold band has been on my finger since she woke up stretched out on my bed like a content cat and with her mouth in a pout. That's our normal; kiss, fuck, and then she eats her breakfast.

"Thank you, your majesty." Turning to Gabby, she winks. "And the vows?"

"Private," we answer in unison, something we both agreed on after setting the date and color scheme. Something my mate was very adamant about—everything must flow and bring good vibes.

The guests could have the rest, but our promises were sacred. Engraved on our rings.

Always and forever.

Nothing else needed to be said.

We are, and will simply always be.

"Then by the power vested—" whatever she said after doesn't matter, nor did we ask if anyone objected. If they did, it would never matter because I'm already kissing my queen, caging her delicate face in my hands while she grips onto the lapels of my tuxedo jacket.

The world fades away, the cheers of those present nothing but a light hum in the background as I lose myself in her taste. How she nibbles my top lip, licking after each drag of her teeth.

"I love you, Gabriella Astor. Nothing in this world matters more than you."

"Always and forever."

"It's you and me."

***

WE FIND the exit as soon as the ceremony's over, leaving our family and guests behind to celebrate as they choose. Stay or go, it doesn't matter to me as I rush out, bride in my arms and a surprise destination in sight.

Gabriella isn't aware of my intentions or plans, but she's giddy as I give her something she's never experienced before: running with me. At top speed, I take off through the dense forest surrounding my land and head north where I own a cottage in the middle of nowhere.

No vampires. No species of any kind.

Just us and nature for the next few nights, no clothing involved.

"Where are we going?" Her question is low, but I hear her as I veer slightly to the right, dodging a tree stump and cut-down log. "Can we leave just like that?"

"A surprise, and yes, we can." Tero and the others have precise instructions, letting Veltross believe that he's in charge while I'm away. My trust in him is gone, as is my patience with his way of thinking. "Besides, we're almost there. Unless you don't feel like spending some quality time alone with your husband."

"I do."

"Good girl."

Nuzzling into my neck for a second, she bites my chin. "Not always good."

"Is that so?"

"You'll have to uncover your present to see."

"Pretty girl," I growl out, my hand fisting the bottom of her dress. "Don't tempt me."

"Not until we get there. You will undress me slowly, no rush."

"Then behave."

"I make no promises." And that's what she does until we arrive, crossing the threshold of a cozy home she pays no mind to. Her sole focus is me and whatever skin she can reach. Each kiss is torture. Each feel of her tongue is heaven. "Have I told you how handsome you looked today? So delicious."

"Look at me," I demand, but instead, my wife tilts her head while running a finger across my jaw. "Gabriella."

"No."

"Please."

Green eyes look up at me from beneath long lashes, her cheeks a little flushed. "Yes."

"This is all your fault."

"What is?" Her feet meet the ground a second before her dress does, yet I'm the one left surprised as I cup her mound. She's bare. Completely. The triangle of well-trimmed hair no longer exists, and now I'm left with smooth skin and the glistening slickness of her cunt.

I drop to my knees, my mouth pressed against her throbbing clit while she trembles, her body reacting to the pleased purr of her mate as I take her scent deep into my lungs. *Motherfuck,* she smells of sweet cream and berries, the scent stronger today than usual and when my tongue laps at her lips and up again, I groan.

The feel of her is different on my mouth, so smooth and soft.

My hunger is ferocious, as if I were a deprived animal, and I slam her against the nearest wall before lifting her, Gabriella's legs on either side of my shoulders, her pussy open and so pink.

"Theo, baby—"

"Feed me. Come on my tongue." Licking my wife from entrance to clit and back again, I swallow every drop of wetness that seeps from her small hole. I marvel at the way she clenches on the tip of my tongue, trying to pull it in deeper while her mouth begs for my cock. "Give me what's mine, Gabriella."

"Make me bleed." Three words. They cause a literal snap in me.

My fangs break through the gums and then her flesh, slicing across the area above her clit without puncturing deep. It won't turn her, but I give her what she craves. The slight pain and then pleasure of the cut before and after I suck, taking in deep pulls of her life's essence.

It's the sweetest treat. No other blood has or will ever satiate me as hers does.

Back arching, my mate uses my tongue in search of her release. The sanguine drops mix with her juices, creating the most intoxicating taste and I take as much of her tiny cunt into my mouth and purr, the loud vibrations settling where she needs me—throbs for me most—and I'm rewarded with the first of her orgasms tonight.

"Baby!" Another harsh tremor rocks her body and her eyes close; I take the opportunity to rid myself of all clothing and my shoes, leaving them somewhere behind us as I turn from the wall and walk deeper into the home. Her cut is starting to close, my saliva healing it, but I clean up the last few drops—force another small crest on her. "I'm sensitive. Give me a moment."

I don't.

I'm too hard.

Sliding her down my body, I poise her over my cock.

"Fuck, pretty girl." With my hands at her hip, I nudge her still-clenching entrance with the head of my cock before sliding in deep in one smooth stroke. "You fit like a glove. So tight. So perfect."

"Gods, what you—"

"No God. Just me, Gabriella." The living room is in front of us, the couch so tempting, but I bounce her instead where I stand, thrusting in and out a few times and then pause. "Say my name."

"Theodore." A plea. A mantra. So sweet.

"Open your eyes for me. Can you do that?" The hooded greens are tired, a bit unfocused, but they do as I ask and take in the living space. "This is my gift to you. A private little sanctuary for when you become overwhelmed and need a break from life at the castle. I had it updated to fit what I thought you might like."

From the soft angles in the furniture and plenty of books to my love of the color black, it melds our two styles perfectly while still being warm and comfortable.

"I love it."

"I'm glad you do." Next, I walk us into the kitchen, rocking her softly as I do. "Simple. Just the basics, but I'll make sure you're fully stocked while here."

She clenches at that, almost violently, and I turn us into a wall. Her legs around me tighten and ankles cross as best they can behind my back. "It's beautiful."

"No. *You* are beautiful; this is all just material."

"But it's your thoughtfulness that makes it so." She moans, gripping my shoulder when I pull out until just the tip is inside and then slam in, her wetness coating us both. Then again. I ride her fast and hard, my hips a punishing blur while she can do nothing but hang onto as best she can.

The noises her pussy makes are addictive.

Yet, I hold myself still on the next punch of my hips and move us from the wall beside the kitchen and toward the bedroom, bypassing the bed to show her the bathroom first. The stark white is bright and clean, spacious enough to fit a large clawfoot tub and walk-in shower that faces the lush backyard which you can see from the floor-to-ceiling windows.

I don't need to ask what she thinks of this room. The approval is in the rush of wetness coating my cock and balls. Our room is next, a large bed at the center with a high, gauzy canopy and four sturdy posts that I'll one day tie her to.

It's all hers.

I'm all hers.

"Thank you, Theo. This is perfect for us."

"It is, but the best is outside that door." She shivers at that, her arms now around my neck. Each step forces me in deeper, my hands on her hips guiding the rest. For every in, I pull out, and when we cross over the threshold and onto the small deck, I lift and then place her feet on the floor facing the railing.

Nothing but trees and foliage surround this property, nature and its peaceful luxury indulging us.

It's what she needs. What her species demands.

To always be outside and one with creation.

"Hands on the rail and feet spread." My pretty girl tries to turn her head, to meet my eyes, but I fist her hair and hold her in place. She gets the pretty interior, and I've earned myself a nice, slick fuck outside. "This won't be gentle, love. I'll take care of you after."

"Please."

"Always and forever." With that I slide in and bottom out, the head of my cock bumping her cervix from this angle. I've been careful with her after our first time, gave her time to rest. To mourn. To trust me to never hurt her.

But now, I'll take care of the side of her no one will ever experience but me: her pleasure.

"Yes," she hisses, undulating her hips to meet me thrust for thrust. Like this, she draws out every inch—tries to control the tempo, but one slap to her thigh remedies that. The crack is loud, but so is the following scream of ecstasy. "So close, Theo."

"Just feel."

"I need more."

"You need what I give you." And I do just that, forcing my cock through her tiny passage with unrelenting speed until she's on the tip of her toes. For each whimper I speed up, for each demand I bring us down until she cries, body strummed tight and just the smallest punch forward makes her shake. "Always trust me to know your body and take care of your needs. Your desires and wants are my priority."

Bringing my thumb to my lips, I lick the tip and then circle her back entrance. For a second, she tenses, not in fear or the thought of pain, but because she likes it. Knows she can come from the slightest touch there.

Something unintelligible comes from her, but I focus on my

shallow thrust and the clenching of her back entrance. The ring of muscle gives way there and she moans, her legs weak.

She wants more.

She wants to feel me stretch her ass.

"Spread yourself for me." Gabriella does as I ask. Reaching back, she parts her cheeks and offers her last virgin hole. It's a dark, rosy pink, so small and tight. "You're the only heaven I'll ever experience, and the home I'll come back to each night. I love you."

"I love you, too."

I'm wet from her juices, but it's not enough and I let a string of my spit fall over the puckered hole and spread it with my engorged head. Each pass goes in a little deeper, her body relaxing under my touch until the head slips in and she freezes, a pain-filled whine leaving the back of her throat.

"Do you want me to stop?"

"More."

"Does it hurt?"

"Sensitive. It tingles," Gabby gets out from between clenching teeth. "I'm so close it hurts."

"Then let me take care of you." One hand gripping her hair and the other on her hip, I push inside the fisting channel until I've bottomed out. The muscle of nerves doesn't stop its contractions, clenching in time with the pulse of her heart.

"Fuck me."

"With pleasure." There's no holding back or pausing to see if she can handle me. However, Gabriella proves just how much of a perfect match we are when reaching back, nails digging into my hip, she urges me to keep moving. She's right at the precipice, just wanting to fall. "Come for me. Now, pretty girl."

The hand on her hip travels to her pussy and cups her as I stroke in and out, dragging every ridge against her sensitive walls, then slam back in. The cadence of our flesh meeting is a beautiful symphony accompanied by the cries of pleasure of my mate.

Pretty girl comes for me on the fourth punch of my hips, her pussy bathing my hand in her wetness while the tightening of her hole milks my cock with constant pulses. She truly is my heaven.

Immediately after the last tremor leaves her body, she's limp and fighting to keep her eyes open. *Adorable.* Picking her up, I carry us back inside and straight for the tub to relax a bit. The warm water and the scent of berries fills the room; I bought this bubble bath because it reminds me of her.

Always sweet. Juicy.

I sit with her between my legs and enjoy the peace she brings.

No noise. No one needing anything from me.

That is, until my sleepy-eyed mate looks back at me from over her shoulder. *Dangerous creature.* "That was the most amazing tour of a home, my love. Does the showing of the grounds come with the same service?"

"Any time you want." Can't help but smirk. So much one can do while out in the open and alone.

Roleplay for one.

"Good." Then she gets a pensive look. "And how long is this—"

"Three days."

"Seventy-two hours without interruptions?"

"Yes."

"Gods, you're perfect."

Gabriella

"A glorified necromancer as the bride of the vampire king. I never thought I'd see the day the monarchy stooped so low," a male voice I'm now very familiar with says, entering the library where I'm relaxing. We've been home two months now, and I'm acclimating myself between my duties here and back home where Leo and Uncle Roberto are working on his magic.

It took a while for me to forgive him, but I get it now.

Just as Isabella's hands were tied, so were his, and that was the dying wish of our father. If Roberto meddled, we would've stayed on our land and trouble would've landed on our doorstep. Be it the fae king or others, we'll never know because we didn't interfere. Many are alive because of that.

However, there are days when I still wonder if Uncle did the right thing or made it worse, but then Theo walks into the room and life calms—finds purpose again. This is the path that fate set out, and I must follow it.

Like now when all I want is a bit of peace and quiet. I'm tired, cranky, and miss Theo, which leads to a volatile little sorceress. I've had a busy morning so far, dealt with a problem back home, and dealing with this imbecile is the last thing I want.

"What can I do for you, General Veltross?" My tone is bored, and my facial expression holds annoyance. I tolerate him as much as he likes me. "As you can see, I'm busy."

"You don't belong here. Your kind is an abomination I'd have eradicated if—"

"You'll never sit on that throne no matter how much you whine about it."

"And he'll never change you. I'll make sure of it." It takes everything in me not to react like he wants; I know he wants a fight, but ire doesn't win wars. Clear thinking does. "My daughter is the rightful queen, and you'll only live long enough to see it."

How long has he been grooming her for this? Feeding her these lies?

"I'm sure you'll try." Standing from my seat on the couch, I take the steps between us and stand toe to toe. I will never be intimidated by this man who reeks of narcissism and greed. "But keep in mind that I'm a firm believer in a hand for a hand. And while you have fangs and sharp nails, I can take a life with a few simple words and the touch of my fingers. Do not threaten me."

"Those things won't work once you're dead."

"They will when I come back. And I will," I say with a saccharine-sweet tone. "My deal with the devil is sealed in my enemies' blood, and I deliver on my promises. Never threaten me again."

He opens his mouth to reply, but my husband enters the room. I know he heard most, if not all, and the tightness in his jaw shows he's holding back, but just barely. "Is there a problem here?" Theo isn't asking me, and I don't volunteer an answer, choosing instead to retake my seat. "Veltross?"

"None at all, my king. Just chatting with—"

"You have nothing to speak about with my mate, General. Learn that quickly."

"Yes, my lord."

"Leave." Veltross walks out stiffly, his footsteps loud and then faint the further away he gets until nothing. Theo's eyes narrow at me, lips in a thin line. "Why can't I end him again? Why not be done with it?"

"Because I think he's our rat and the way to figure out Larue's next move."

"Are you sure?"

"I am." Handing over the invitation to Larue's home; I watch his face as he reads. From anger to amusement and then to that cockiness I adore, my husband doesn't disappoint. "How grand of the king to offer a dinner in our honor."

"Yes, but more importantly, Tero saw the messenger and Veltross together. Your general received a large sum of money along with that letter, which he singlehandedly delivered to me."

THREE DAYS LATER, we find ourselves on foreign soil and in a kingdom where the subjects either looked scared or full of piss and vinegar. No in-between or even a normal serious disposition.

Yet, King Larue seems jovial and enthused at our arrival.

My sister is also here, along with her mate.

There are a few representatives of each army: vampire, werewolf, and Wiccan here. But going by his expression, you'd say he doesn't get much outsider company, good or bad, and this is nowhere near a social visit.

"Welcome, friends. We are all so pleased to have you—"

"Cut the bullshit and get to the point. I've never been one for small talk, and you know this."

In the blink of an eye, the niceties are gone. This is the man who's taken so much from me and my family: our parents, our people, our security and peace. He's evil, I see that clear as day now, but there's something else behind his bitter eyes and when they meet mine, it's all there.

Larue is afraid of something. Absolutely terrified.

"What have you done?" At my question, his eyes widen but he's quick to school his features. Some might have missed it, those of fae heritage in the room, but those with me see it all. "Who are you trying to dissuade or appease?"

"Mind your tongue, woman. You're before a king."

"And you before a queen and the werewolves' luna. Do not confuse us with the females of your kingdom."

"Theodore, I suggest—"

"My mate asked you a question."

"How can you accept such insolence?" *He's baiting us to react.* "Women have no place in this negotiation. They are to be seen and not heard."

"Is that why your mate left you?" Xadiel steps in beside me with my sister on his other side. Our family is mix-matched, but a united front. "Why you're so bitter, old friend?"

"We're not here to discuss my personal life, but that which you have that belongs to me."

"And what is that?" Theo lifts my hand and kisses each knuckle. "Be specific."

"My son," Larue grits out. Those in his guard draw their weapons then, taking a step forward.

Are we surprised by this? No. Are we intimidated? Also, no.

Which is why Tero enters the room in his snake form a few minutes later dragging an unconscious royal with his mouth. His son has been kept dirty, unfed, and his wings were clipped.

"This is the only warning you'll receive," my husband growls out as Tero lifts his head over the son of a man not worthy of his crown. "Stand down, Larue. Do not come near our mates or their people unless you want a war on your hands you will never win. With your greed and idiocy, you've brought together three factions that want your head on a spike for the village dogs to piss on, and who will stop at nothing to do so."

"I'm not afraid of you."

"Want to test that theory as my trusted guard suffocates your son? Or while he swallows him, head first?"

"You wouldn't dare." Many inside gasp—his people—their eyes bouncing between their useless leader and Theo. They wait for orders that will never come. "That's an act of war."

"It is."

"Is she worth it? The death of your people?"

Tero's teeth scrape over the royal son's forehead.

"Last chance."

Larue is sweating, hands clenching at his sides as Tero unlocks his jaw. "Stop."

"Smart man." The python recedes, taking a stance in front of me, and the fae king's eyes narrow.

"Can my son be removed and attended to?"

"Yes." The fact I'm the one who answers further angers him. "You may."

For a few minutes, he doesn't say anything. Just looks at me. "You have it, don't you?" he asks, less acerbic and more understand-ing, which throws me for a loop. *What is wrong with this man?* "It's why you're so confident?"

"Have what?"

"Ask your sister. She knows." My head turns to Isa who looks ahead, body showing no sign of outward deceit, yet I know he's right. For someone so angered by this man's greed, today she's subdued, hiding behind the wall that is her mate. "Just know that I'm not the only one interested. Many will come for you both."

"Isa?"

"Not now, sister. We must go home." And it's the urgency in her voice, the tremor, that has me follow her while our mates walk behind us. Something is wrong.

Why do I feel as though we've lost?

Gabriella

His hand is on the small of my back as we follow the hostess to our table. We've been married for four months now, a peaceful time where King Larue has kept true to his word and has gone silent along with Isabella. She's avoiding our pending conversation, refuses to say more than there's an amulet residing inside of me and her.

My gift is from death.

Hers is from mother earth.

The beginning and end.

To see beyond what's in front of you.

That's it. Nothing else.

And I'm angry at her for staying quiet for so long.

Yet, there's also peace in my soul since this ended. No more hunting my kind or looking over our shoulders; our people have also become more tolerant of each other and accept that change can be a beautiful thing.

We all love the same.

We all mourn the same.

Together, we are unstoppable.

Maybe it's time to revisit the topic of changing me? Maybe that's why Isabella finally sent word yesterday that we'll meet tomorrow.

The young woman in front of us sways her hips, trying to garner the attention of every man in the room, and yet fails miserably. Pathetically so, yet something about her is familiar to me and I feel an irrational bout of anger run through my veins.

I don't know her, but the hate inside me is unmistakable.

I'm embarrassed for her. I giggle through our recently discovered mind link—our sacred bond that after the last full moon morphed into something deeper—and Theo chuckles, amused by my candor. But then again, I'm always nothing but honest, that breath of fresh air in his frozen lungs.

His dead heart beats for me. His darkness surrounds me in warmth.

"Humans are disrespectful by nature." My voice is low, but he nods, and I know she heard, the subtle stumble telling me as much. His face holds a bit of disgust, too. He hates to be around mortals, but tonight we came here for me. To celebrate a human holiday because I find the idea of Valentine's Day quite adorable. That, and he loves his macabre gift of a steel blade he can attach to the end of his finger like a claw. It's silly, totally unnecessary for a vampire, but it inspired him to make a reservation for this romantic dinner.

"They hold no qualms in trying to bed a taken male or female, my love. No honor. No code."

"That they are," I say as he pulls me a little closer, his arm wrapping around my midsection. His need to feel skin on skin rivals mine, and I sigh when he places a chaste kiss on the nape of my neck.

The hostess leads us to a table set for two near the back with the dark night sky as our backdrop. The windows are open, and the moon is high—the stars light up the dark abyss above while I sit in the chair he pulls out for me. We ignore the hostess and her idiocy.

The placement of my husband's menu across the table and away from me is not lost on either of us.

Nor is her scent. The differences that let her fit in amongst those in the city.

"Is this table to your liking, sir?" the woman asks, moving closer to his side, but before she can place a hand on my mate's arm, he has her wrist in his hold. Had we been anywhere else, he wouldn't hesitate to rip it off, but for now I'm satisfied by the subtle crunch of bones and her yelp. "Sir, you're—"

"Never touch me," my husband hisses out, the command of a king, eyes flashing red while she begins to shake. His fangs descend for a second, piercing the gums while she watches in fear. "Disrespect my wife again, and I'll have your head on a spike outside the palace walls. Now, go back to the front and don't come back."

"My apologies."

"Not accepted, hybrid."

"How?" the hostess asks me while holding her wrist against her chest, voice trembling. She knew who we were. "No one here—"

"Silence." Her immediate compliance to my demand is false, belittled by her earlier behavior. Stupid and idiotic; I study her for a few minutes, stretching out the silence while she shifts nervously, a whimper escaping her. "Name."

"Elise."

"Elise what?"

"Veltross. My name is Elise Veltross." Even though half human, her essence is reminiscent of his. Earthy, but mixed with roses to enhance her femininity. Moreover, her father's words the day Theo fought the young and moronic vampire who challenged him still ring in my head.

"You will never be one of us, witch. The king will soon become bored with you and toss you aside as he's done with his lovers in the past." The haughty expression on his face angered me, but more than that is his audacity to insult his king himself and his privacy.

I know my mate is not a virgin.

I don't expect a man his age—who's lived through centuries and watched the world evolve—to be one, but Veltross's blatant contempt and arrogance is grating on my nerves. The way he mocks our bond isn't something I can easily let go of.

Not here. Theo needs to focus.

Breathing in and out, I plaster a fake smile across my lips. "And let me guess—you have the perfect woman for him in mind? Or are you in love with your king?"

"Don't be insolent, child."

"Don't push me, you backward-thinking fool. My patience is thin." *My sister finally catches on, moving closer, and I shake my head at her, a minute movement she sees and proceeds to fist the back of my dress, tugging me closer and in front of her so she doesn't react.* *"Leave. This is your only warning."*

"The day my daughter takes her rightful place, I'll take great pleasure in draining every drop of blood from your veins."

"The day your daughter crosses my path, she should watch her back. I'm not one to be messed with."

"And what will you do? Your cheap tricks don't—"

"That tugging you feel at your chest is the black soul that resides in you. I can manipulate it, turn it against you, Veltross. That pain will be magnified, and it will be I who dances on your grave."

"The daughter of one of my generals. One who would be embarrassed by your behavior and punish you just as swiftly." *Coincidence, or...?* my mate asks through our link, tilting his head while studying her. *Have you spoken to Isabella?*

"Yes." Eyes on the ground, Elise takes a step back. "I'm very sorry."

We're to meet tomorrow afternoon. "You let your human side overpower and disgrace our very nature and laws, Miss Veltross." Eyes narrowed, I watch her through slits while clutching the napkin in my hand. I'm not buying her sudden contrite act, nor do we trust her father. He's a good general but thinks too highly of himself and his position. His actions toward me have put a mark on his back. "How dare you try and touch my mate and your king."

It's in her body language. A part of her has a misplaced claim on him; I scent her jealousy.

"I was being—"

"You speak when spoken to. Understood?"

"Yes, My queen."

"Do not step a single foot out of line, Elise. This is my only warning."

"Yes, My queen."

"Leave."

"Thank you, My queen." Elise scurries off and doesn't look back, hiding up front while I'm served dinner by an older gentleman and my husband watches me eat. It's something he enjoys, to sit and quietly observe while I return the favor when he hunts—when he lets nature take its rightful place and he momentarily satiates the never-ending thirst.

My king has great control over his impulses. He only kills to eat, as any hunter would do.

It's sexy to watch him overpower his prey.

My thighs clench under the table at the memory of his meal last night, the beauty of his brutality, an action my husband catches. His nostrils flare and his eyes become darker—hooded and hungry. A little feral, and I lick the last bite of my dessert sensually from the spoon.

A move he follows with a different, unrestrained hunger.

"Two minutes, Gabriella."

"Two minutes?" I ask, feigning an ignorance that makes him flash those sharp fangs at me. "Run, pretty girl."

"I'm not afraid of you," I taunt, leaning over to nip his jaw. "Now close your eyes and count to sixty. Come find me if you can."

"Are you challenging your king?"

"Always, love. Always."

ALL DAY there's been a heaviness at the center of my chest weighing me down. It's this feeling of foreboding that won't leave me alone, as if something is coming and it can't be undone.

Death looms, calls to me, and he demands my attention.

It's never been like this. So omnipotent.

What does it want?

"I wish Theo was here." My whisper to the empty bedroom echoes, bouncing off the walls in a taunting manner, and the claustrophobic feeling of being trapped squeezes at my throat. "What the hell is going on?"

Not that I get an answer. If anything, the sensation intensifies, and I stumble out of the chair I'd been sitting on. I'm unsteady and breathing hard, and nothing matters more than leaving this room.

There's no one in the hall when I leave, yet Marcia and Meera appear almost instantly by my side. Both watch me with worry in their eyes. They feel it. Something is off.

"Take me to the fields. I need to wait to see Theo."

"He and Tero aren't back yet, Gabby." Meera tries to steer me toward the room, but I shake her and Marcia off, her snake not fully healed from her change. "Please. Let's just wait in the room."

"No." I'm shaking my head as the walls around me seem to close in. "I can't be indoors."

"Okay." Meera holds two hands up. "We'll just walk with you."

"Thank you." It takes minutes to reach the open air, and at once a bit of the tension eases. "I think I had a panic attack in there. My senses are off, and everything feels as though I have a hundred fire ants crawling under my skin."

"You'll be fine. Just slowly inhale and then out." Following her instructions, I gather myself and regulate my breathing, taking some control back. Not that it fully heals me, but I'm more myself by the five-minute mark—and very parched. Inexplicably so. "Thirsty?"

"How did you know?" Marcia takes off in the general direction of the kitchen.

"Because while locked up in that prison my father built, I lived through many of those episodes. It'll pass, but you will be very tired —weak for a few days after."

"Okay."

"Just stay here. I'll be right back…it'll be faster if I help her."

Nodding, I close my eyes and focus on my breathing. I'm alone maybe a few minutes tops, when a presence looms over me. His scent is irritating.

"Now is not the time, General. I'm not in the mood for one of our special talks."

"I had your father killed, witch."

My eyes snap open at that, the feeling from before hitting me full force and I almost stagger back. "What did you just say?"

"I'm the reason your parents are dead, and I'm going to enjoy ending you." Veltross sneers, so much malice in his eyes, while in his hand is a large blade I've never seen before. It's sharp and old, the steel glinting in the early dusk lighting. Those closest to us had no time to react. Even with their speed, it was too late when at first our conversation seemed normal: a general addressing his superior regarding a private matter.

That should've been the first clue. How stupid could I be?

But then Isabella's words from her note hit me in the chest right as the tip of his blade embeds deep into my heart. Every word slices deeper than the sharp steel ever could.

I'm sorry, but everything will be as it should.

But why? Why have me fall in love, only to leave him behind in absolute agony?

The pain spreads through me quickly, my blood saturating the fabric of my dress as yells rend the air. Something was on that blade; the sudden weakness in my limbs doesn't give me a second to catch my breath or heal myself—it's all too fast. I stumble, and hands grab me. They're on my face and others on my upper body, but I can't make anything out.

It hurts. My heart breaks for the man I'll never get to truly enjoy loving.

To have a family with.

"Gabby, please!" Louder, a shout. A woman. Several. Then men, but soon all noises become muffled while a comforting presence wraps its cold skin around my leg. *Marcia.* I try to reach out to her mind, but nothing.

My connection with her is full of static—as is the one I hold with Theo.

I'm slipping away without a chance to ask for help. To tell him I'll be okay.

I'll always love you, my King.

Vampire King
THEODORE ASTOR

"Bring him to me." The guards stand and drag a kicking, screaming Veltross to me. They toss him at my feet and step back.

"My king, I—"

"Stand up, General."

"Please, listen to me." When I don't reply, he shifts a bit, looking for an out. To his bad luck, he's being blocked by the same men he's trained and led into battle. They are an impenetrable wall. "I did what I did for you. Our people deserve—"

He's cut off by my hand on this throat, lifting him off the ground. He thrashes, tries to remove my fingers, but I walk us to where Gabriella lies, her back supported by Tero. And my wife, she's pale and her chest is red, a large gash crossing from side to side. It's deep. She's lost too much blood for me to seal the wound. *He bled her.* "I will never marry your daughter."

"She's better—"

"You and your offspring will die by my blade, no matter how

197

long it takes." My hand squeezes, and for each staggered breath my wife takes, I tighten my hold. With my other, though, I puncture his abdomen with the use of my nails, tearing out chunks at a time. His side. His dead organs. His bones.

I don't stop until the bottom half of his body is on the floor, and his chest with the head attached is all that's left.

"Dad!" Elise screams suddenly, rushing to where we are, but Meera flings her back and across the yard. She lands awkwardly and is knocked unconscious, yet no one checks on her. I also didn't realize Meera's set up to work. She has herbs and crystals surrounding Gabriella.

Did Tero call her?

Or Gabriella?

"We need to bind her soul, Theo," Meera says from beside me, her hand on my shoulder. "We don't have a lot of time. End him now, and I'll do everything in my power to bring her back."

Her pleading gives me breath, but the pain I'm experiencing intensifies when her eyes close. My wife's chest still rises and falls, but those gems I love no longer have the energy to meet mine.

"You will never be a part of the royal family," I snarl, holding him at eye level.

"Please stop. You will be so much—"

"Your children will never amount to anything, Veltross. Will be nothing but outcasts in my kingdom." With that, I rip his head off and toss it aside, leaving it for the guards to clean while I rush to my wife. Her body's shaking as I pull her gently against my chest, tears running down from closed lids, and I've never felt more useless in my life.

I'm the king, and yet I can't save the one person in this world I breathe for.

Meera whispers something in her ear, and the only sign of life is the small squeeze of my hand that's barely perceptible. And I hold on to that moment, close my eyes, and control my body as a sob rocks me, my body covering hers as the last breath leaves her small frame.

Those around me weep. The sorrowful cries of every vampire can be heard for miles as they feel her connection wane, and then nothing. She's gone. My love is not here.

Throwing my head back, I let out a deafening roar that shakes the ground we stand on. A few windows shatter, and those around me whimper and cower in fear while I crumble as her man.

"Is there anything we can do?" I ask Meera, the sound of my voice sounding foreign. Lifeless.

"I can bind her here; she showed me how to in the past."

"But…" I pull Gabriella a little tighter against me, my face buried against my mark—the first tattoo came in the day our mind link slid into place. I kiss it with reverence because she'll always be my gift. Mine.

"I can't predict when she'd be back. Her soul will belong to this world, but not her body until death decides otherwise." I can smell Meera's tears, and if I could, I'd be bawling like a child myself. My heart feels broken, although it doesn't beat. My soul feels ruptured, and existing in a world where she no longer walks isn't something I can do. We either walk side by side, or leave this life together. My world has been in her pretty little hands since the day we met. "I'm so sorry, my king. Only she can take and give life."

My face snaps to hers, my chest heaving harshly as the beast within rattles the cage and thirsts, for vengeance. To kill. "Do it." Standing from the ground, I lay my beauty down and then place a tiny kiss across the cupid's bow of her lips. "Do whatever you must. No matter the cost."

***

SEVENTY-TWO HOURS PASS, and the sun never rises.

It's total darkness, and my vampires sob for their fallen queen. No matter how little time she had with us, those who are loyal to the crown came to love her as I do.

Her beauty. Her heart.

She is the purest and most beautiful soul.

"It's time, my king." Tero places a hand on my arm and I nod, walking behind him to the tribute made by the elders in her honor. We know a minute tendril of her soul lingers—she'll mostly reside where my father does—and yet those here will continue to sense Gabriella.

I can still smell her. Taste her in the air around me.

But the pain is just the same when you can't hug or kiss the one you love.

Is this what you lived with, pretty girl—this agonizing hollowness that never ceases the torture?

All who I pass bow their heads, their sobs echoing across the land. The cadence is full of pain, a mere tenth of what I'm choking on, but comfort is out of my reach.

Nothing will ever make this better than having her again, a hope I'm clinging to.

Her family is here, yet I refuse to speak to any of them.

Gabriella went above the line of loyalty for them. She defended and loved, yet Isabella's avoidance after the meeting with Larue cut my wife deep. She wouldn't say it, but I saw it in her eyes each time she'd fail to connect with her sister.

It was there when her uncle explained his reasons for abandoning them.

When Marcia got hurt, and she nearly killed herself to save a friend.

Every time she gave it was honest and pure, yet life didn't always reciprocate in kindness.

That's why I ignore everyone and slip inside the coffin with my mate before the casket is lowered. They will not be taking her body back to the Moore's mausoleum; she will remain where I can see her, talk to her—care for the place she rests while her body and spirit recharge to come back.

Today. A week. Years from now.

Doesn't matter; I will wait for my queen to rise once more.

The dirt covers her coffin, and soon the cries of many turn to muffled noises that I pay no heed to. And the longer we lay there—the longer I go without feeding—I find my quiet. Brodej and Tero will step in and take care of any coven needs while I visit someone who owes me.

Hunger gives way to madness, my grief and needs too strong to contain, but I do.

I bring myself to death's door to be by the side of my queen as my father calls her back.

Her spirit has been waiting for me, and when I awake to a hand in mine, it's her face that greets me with a smile. "Hi."

"Hello, pretty girl."

"You're handsome. Has anyone ever told you that?"

"Someone once did, but they're here, and I'm all alone missing her."

Gabriella's lips purse. "Is she worth it? Because I'd never leave you."

"Come along, my child. My son and I need to speak." He's here, and although I want to bash his head into the nearest wall, I can't look away. Who knows when I'll see her again. "Do you want him to visit you after?"

"I do. Your son is cute."

"Then he will." My wife walks away then, her spirit lighter, *too bright for this place* as she walks through a wall and out of my sight. "Speak."

"Bring her back," I snarl, my chest exploding with a mixture of pain and love too large to contain. "You are the only one who can, Thanatos. Do it. For the first time in your miserable existence, do something that's not self-serving."

"I'm sorry, son. This has to happen."

"So you want me to relive your story? To lose the woman I love like you lost my mother."

His tall figure cloaked in black looks at me with pity, his own sorrow coming through clear as day. "If there was another way, I'd do it. I'm the giver of death, not life, and asking for this kind of favor comes with a heavy price."

"Our future children."

"As of right now, my grandchildren will never be."

Right now? I'd ponder that later because there's something more important to ask.

"How could you give her to me and then take her away? Why?"

"Please understand that this is how it must be to save the future of all species. You two are the balance while her sister is the heart, and her mate will remain her compass. Without balance, there is no heart or direction, and all will be lost. Your wife will be back; I promise, my son. Gabriella has always been and will remain yours."

"When?"

"When the enemy shows his hand once more." Closing the distance between them, Thanatos grabs my arms and marks the inside of my wrists. I've felt this pain before. Years ago, when I received the first ones on my back and chest. Only then does my father meet my eyes. "I've never wanted you to experience what it's like to live without your mate. This is where I've failed you the most, but there is one thing I can do to ease the pain. Once a year, on her birthday, you can come and spend the day together until she is reborn. There is no expiration date on this; just never stop fighting for her."

With that he's gone, and I look down at my new tattoos.

By blood and pact. You are one.

PLEASE READ

IF YOU HAVE NOT READ LITTLE LIES…

This is where I tell you to pause if spoilers are not your thing and
pick up the first book. There is a reason this story was told
backwards, and I wouldn't want to spoil it for you.

Happy Reading!

Now, if you don't care and are like me…go for it and breathe.

It will all make sense soon.

Elena XoXo

Epilogue #1
KING

"**M**y Lord, it's time," Tero hisses, his body stumbling into the room while his hands shake, so unlike his usual composed behavior. There's a slim file in his grip. His poise is gone while his eyes turn lighter and snake-like as his body vibrates from across my desk. "You've patiently been waiting for this day to come."

He's nervous. Excited. Half-shifted as his lower body begins to unveil his animal; a large albino constrictor that's the complete opposite of his stubborn sibling. Slithering a little closer, his trembling hand places the manila folder atop my desk, his smile wide and mischievous.

"What has you in such a good mood, Tero? Are you okay?"

"Just look, my king. Please."

I nod and look down, my finger opening the front flap, and then I freeze. Every muscle in my body locks down and my dead heart thumps harshly inside my chest. A part of me that's been gone for so long—emotions I've buried deep—they all hit me at once when her smiling face greets me on a 4x6 picture paper-clipped to a bio/resume.

It's her. My pretty girl after all these years.

By blood and pact, we've always been one.

The tears don't fall, yet the pain of losing her all those years ago strikes me with a vengeful hatred, tearing me apart as if I'm watching the light fade from the gorgeous green eyes all over again. She bled out in my arms. Her last breath was against my chest.

However, none of it matters now.

Instead, I'm smiling. My body thrums with excitement and want, a thankful exhale rushing through my chest because she's here once again. Meera's promise, their sacred magic, and Thanatos's word have gifted me the only thing that's ever truly mattered.

And while my father did allow me to visit her spirit while in the land of fire before her rebirth, it was never enough.

I've waited for a hundred years to kiss her.

I've been patient since we identified her with certainty thirteen years ago; denying myself the privilege of so much as being close. I couldn't interfere. This was her path back to me and I had to grit my teeth and allow it.

That all ends today.

"Her birthday is within the next month. We must prepare."

Tero's eyes narrow then and his top lip curls. "Elise might be a problem."

"She won't." I won't let her. My eyes shift to the Stygian blade on my wall, and I smirk; the enemy has risen, and I will take great pride in delivering the same treatment they gave my wife. A thousand cuts over.

I might have bided my time and played in the background, unable to interfere without breaking my end of the pact, but that doesn't mean Gabriella is alone. Meera and Tero are never far, they provide what I directly can't, and Elise is playing the part I need her to.

Veltross might be dead, but there are others who think like he did.

They've scattered like roaches. They've spread throughout the world, but for the last six months many have been congregating outside of Seattle.

Ignorant fools.

I know each move they make. I move the pieces in this game of chess to my amusement.

They will strike, and I will be there to end it all at once. No mercy. No one from the bloodline will remain untouched.

"Dial Elise for me and put her through. It's time we hunt."

"As you wish, my lord." Picking up the phone on my desk, he does just that and then puts it on speakerphone. It rings a few times, no more than three, and then there's heavy breathing on the other end meant to entice. As if she's exerting herself.

"Hello," Elise says, her tone breathy and exaggerated. "This is Elise Scott."

Did she really think a change of name would be enough for me to forget? Imbecile. "Miss Scott, this is Theodore Astor with Astor Galleries. How are you today?"

"Mr. Astor!" Her high pitch makes Tero gag, and I bite back a chuckle. "So nice to hear from you. How can I help you?"

"This is about a Gabriella Moore."

"Oh." Less cheerful. A little acerbic.

"Yes, you sent me her portfolio and I must say, her work is exquisite." My pretty girl has always been talented. "Her painting, a warrior's death, is quite provocative and the kind of talent we'd like to acquire for a show. Does she have any openings for this fall?"

"I'd have to check her schedule, but I'm more than willing to meet and discuss a partnership?"

"I'll have my assistant contact you with the details. His name is Tero. Please expect a call."

"Tero, you say."

"I did. Is there a problem?"

"No. Not at all." Fake cheeriness. The tilt in her tone shows she's uncomfortable.

"Good. I look forward to seeing you…" she gasps, and then tries to hide it with a cough "…both." Before she can reply, I cut the call and Tero places the phone back in the cradle. "That went well."

"She's just as stupid now as she was back then."

"Very true." Before sitting back in my chair, I pick up the picture of my wife and admire her. From the fiery red of her hair to the adorable freckles above the bridge of her nose and then those lips, bee-stung and so pink, that I've missed, how could anyone ever forget her?

But then again, cockiness leads to stupidity on its way to failure.

Elise used King Larue's personal mage to cast a spell on me. It was weak and disorganized and had no effect on me or my memories.

You can't control a demon. Not that I told anyone.

Let Elise think otherwise.

It'll make my hunt all the more entertaining.

My pretty girl will remember. She will take her rightful place at my side once again.

Queen Gabriella has risen, and it's time she bathes in the blood of her enemies.

EPILOGUE #2
Queen

For a few days I've been avoiding my husband, and it's not out of spite or anger. If anything, the smile on my face would be a dead giveaway of the light—the new sense of life bursting inside of me.

I know what he's been through. What he gave up to someday love me again, and while I'll forever be thankful, a small part of me still weeps over his despair. He didn't deserve the hand fate dealt us, but trust and loyalty are two prized qualities and thankfully, we've been rewarded with this new life.

"You think he's getting suspicious?" Marcia comes to stand beside me, holding her hand out for the keys to my Mercedes G-Wagon while my sister and Meera leave with their mates. Not that I'm surprised; my snake shifter spent so many years trapped inside her animal's flesh and missed out on a hundred years' worth of progress and innovation. My poor friend watched the world pass by, watched people grow and advance—live—while swallowing back her misery.

Because I know she's suffered.

I feel the longing that at times consumes her soul. The part of me that gave her life once again, merged with her essence, calls out to the universe for two things: a mate, and the experience so many take for granted.

So if Marcia wants to drive, I let her.

"He is, but…" I trail off, pulling my phone from my back pocket. It's a text from Theo.

"But?"

"But not for the right reason. He'd never suspect that I'm—" The phone rings, cutting me off as I try to read what he sent; I don't bite back my smile. This man has no patience at all. Not when it comes to me. "Hello, my King."

"You've been gone long enough," Theo croons low, the deep timbre of his voice flowing over my skin like a sinful caress. "Never again, pretty girl. The next time you and your sister need a *girls' weekend*…" he spits the words out with distaste, and I find the barely contained snarl sexily adorable "…I'll stay a floor below yours and drive you to and from myself. Understood?"

"If you wish."

"I do." Appeased by my agreement, his beast lets out a content purr. A noise that does more than soothe. It calls to the very essence inside of me. "When will you arrive? I'm—"

"Why don't you come and find me?" I challenge, interrupting the pleasant conversation. We're just a few miles from our home here in the outskirts of Seattle, a large plot of land with no other homes for miles. Open terrain where our people—our alliances—can be free without having to bend to fit into human society and their norms. "Do you think you can?"

His chuckle is low and full of hunger. "Run, pretty girl."

"Chase me, King Astor." I hang up the phone then and turn to look over at Marcia. "Drop me off here and bring the car back in a few days. I have a feeling I'll be busy with his majesty."

The car slows down.

Then it comes to a complete stop.

Marcia isn't looking at me, though, and when I follow her line of sight, I'm hit with her emotions. This one is of happiness mixed with wariness and the need to show her dominance. *Oh shit.*

There's a man in a white SUV with the windows rolled down and all-black eyes staring at her. His skin is melding with that of his animal, the pattern of a cobra: black with hints of olive and a bit of brown.

She shakes under his stare, her own black scales showing a bit.

Two cobras. Both are deadly.

"Mate," Marcia whispers, but in the silence of the car's cab, it's loud and imposing. "He's my mate."

"Go to him."

"Don't get out of the—"

My passenger side door is pulled open, and the low snarl that greets my ears has me pouting. "Seriously, you couldn't wait?"

"No." The anger in his tone makes me look at him, yet his attention is not on me but the stranger. The curl of his lip and the thunderous expression is one I've seen before; Veltross and his family were the cause in the past. "Get out and behind me."

"Theo, I need you to calm down. He's her mate."

"I know, but he's a serpentine prime and if he were to attack us, I'd have to kill him."

"Please don't." Marcia's voice is low and meek, yet the excitement is still there. She's needed her other half all these years. "Let me go and talk to him."

"Go." One word, hard, and yet I know he's happy for her.

"Tell Tero that—"

"Go be happy, my sister of the heart."

"Thank you, Gabby." Slowly, the grace of her animal present, Marcia exits the vehicle and walks over. He's waiting for her. His face is full of longing and peace.

However, I don't stay to watch the scene unfold…

Before my husband can stop me, I take off at full speed and barefoot into the lush forest near our home. The wind picks up around me, and the soft brush of leaves under my feet feels good—connects me to the Wiccan heritage that runs through my veins. It feeds me, rejuvenates my soul, and says hello to the little life growing inside of me.

The trees sway for us and the wind surrounds my body, fluttering my hair while the babbling brook creates a lovely melody I hum to as I run.

I know Theo's behind me, hunting, but I still put on a show with my speed, which rivals his. It doesn't take long to reach our estate and the large tree at the center of our backyard that I insisted we bring from Italy. The large red cedar overshadows all other vegetation, standing tall and proud, but more beautiful is the man leaning against it with a cocky expression.

"Couldn't let me win this time?"

"No." He pushes off the base, his gait powerful yet graceful. His nose also flares the closer to me he gets, eyes flicking from amber to a rich ruby red as reality dawns on him. Not that he asks. No, my husband simply walks up to me and then kneels, his hands on each side of my waist.

"Ask me."

"Gabriella, this…please explain." Voice low. So much hope.

"What do you hear? Smell?" A deep rumble builds in his chest, a different kind of purr, and the flutter inside of me accepts the owner. Bringing a hand to his face, I cup his chin and tilt it up slightly, just enough so our eyes meet. "Go on. Tell me."

Theo shakes before me, his fangs down. "I hear a heartbeat and smell honeysuckle."

"And what do you feel?"

"A hope I shouldn't be allowed to."

"That's where you're wrong." I try to drop to his level, but he doesn't allow me to. Instead, I'm picked up and placed to straddle his body that now sits on the ground. We're chest to chest. Stomachs touching. "You also ruined my surprise, you know."

"Did I?"

"You did, but we'll get back to your punishment after." Under me, his cock swells and I bite my lip. *News first. Ride him after.*

"My apologies, pretty girl. I'm yours to do with as you please."

Leaning a little forward, I nip his lip, piercing the skin just a little. The cut is shallow, but the taste of blood—the drop I steal—is like an aphrodisiac. Tastes like mana, and I cherish how we can still do this for the other, because just like him, blood runs through my veins.

He's part god. I'm a hybrid.

Yet our blood has the same consistency. Same taste as before.

And after I've fed, nothing is sexier than giving sustenance to the man I love.

"Now, I want you to get up and walk us back to the tree and to the left side." His grin is amused, a little questioning emotion in his eyes, but Theo does as I ask. We stop beside the huge base. The hand-sized red bow I taped to it before leaving with the girls is still there, and I point to it. "Please remove." Again, no hesitation, and when he does, a small cavern within the tree's trunk is more visible. This hole is just large enough for a hand to slip inside and I tilt my head, nodding at him to get a move on. I'm dying here.

"Baby?" he asks, but I just point and after shaking his head, slips his hand inside. I hear the rattle the moment he grips the small box, and I bite my lower lip to keep it in. The silver paper glints in the sunlight filtering through the branches and leaves: it says *CONGRATS* in a bright and cheery font, but to my husband it means nothing, and he rips it clean off without my suggestion. And I'm clinging to him as he does, keeping the constant contact between my abdomen and his, my arms around his neck.

However, the moment he sees the contents inside, I know everything I did for this miracle is worth it. He swallows hard and for the second time in his life, Theo's infallible control shatters. Ruby eyes meet mine and the look of wonder in them brings tears to my eyes, the red drop slide down my cheek as I nod, confirming what we both know to be true.

One of his hands grips the small onesie in a tight fist while the other wraps around my hair. The hold is tight, but I love it. The way his entire body shivers is sweet agony, and I want him. Now. Always.

"Do you remember when we saw this tiny outfit a year ago?" Our lips hover, and when my back meets the tree's bark, I arch to get closer. Kiss him; once—three times in quick little pecks. "We were in Barcelona and wanted to buy Tero's son something for the travels home. You couldn't stop looking at this one, love. I knew your yearning was as heavy as mine, but those moments cemented it for me."

"How?" Voice hoarse, he reaches over and places the small outfit back in the hole carefully, the rattle on top. It's a black cotton onesie with the words *My Daddy Bites* and two fangs right below in bright red lettering from a Gothic store the locals seem to love; I went back and bought it the next day while he spoke to Tero. It's perfect for us. For our little vamp. "To bring you back, I had to—"

"Your father owed me." At his perplexed expression, I giggle. "He's loved just like you and suffered just the same, but her soul belongs to the Lord of the Underworld. So, I bargained."

"What did you do?"

"I brought her back with the condition that he give to me what he stole as payment."

"And when was this?" There's a touch of accusation there, but awe overrides it. Yes, what I did could've had bad repercussions, but I'd pay anything to give him this. To start our family. "Did he come here?"

My look is sheepish. "Two weeks ago, and no. I went to him in a dream."

"You…" Theo trails off before his nails slice through my top and then shorts. The destroyed scraps of fabric fall to the ground, and I'm left in nothing but a pair of black lace cheekies he picked out on our last shopping trip. No bra, as he tore that one off with the top. My breasts bounce with my gasp at the act, my skin burning hot with need. "You sneaky, devious, and glorious little demon."

"But you love me like this."

"I do. Always have." That growl causes my thighs to clench, and he smirks while lifting his T-shirt off and tossing it aside. "But you know this and like to play dangerous games."

The gusset of my panties is no longer there, but the head of his cock is.

I look down and find his pants are ripped, the area where the zipper and button were completely shredded into useless scraps. "The payoff was worth it."

"It is." Then he's buried inside to the hilt. One smooth stroke, and I'm lost to him. Can't say anything else as he pulls out and slams back in, taking me hard and fast against my favorite tree. The place where he learned he'd become a father in a few months.

My hips move against his, chasing more of the feelings only Theo can evoke.

"I love you," I say against his mouth, undulating to meet his next thrust. This is fast and dirty, not the way most would celebrate becoming parents, but it's us. Later he'll cuddle me and spoil and spend some time nuzzling my stomach, but right now, we need this.

To reconnect. To feel.

"And I'll live for you both, beautiful. Love you harder every day." Releasing my hair, he brings a hand between our bodies and down to where we are joined. He presses two fingers against my clit and holds it there, his heavy cock flexing—dragging against my walls on each thrust. "You are my world, Gabriella. I'm a blessed man to walk this life with you by my side. Humbled that you accept me."

"By blood and pact." It leaves me on a moan as his hips pick up the pace, almost a blur, and my ass bounces, the smack of skin loud in the open air. On the next upward stroke, though, a rush of pleasure strikes me as his mental walls lower and I see through his eyes. Feel the love he has for me. For our child. "Oh, God. Baby, I—"

"We are one." Those words, his truth, it's all too much and I throw my head back as a scream tears from me. My orgasm ripples through me like a bolt of lightning, sharp and unforgiving, but it's nothing like the feel of his teeth in my skin.

Theo bites down over his mark again, embedding his fangs deep, and I can't do anything but hold on tight. Try to find an anchor as he sends me straight into a second orgasm that leaves me boneless. Struggling to breathe, yet the second he comes and his seed covers my walls, I'm at peace.

Home.

We stay like that for a few minutes, just basking and lazily petting, but a small flutter pulls both of our attentions to my stomach. Theo pulls back just enough to look down, the softest expression I've ever seen on his face while his hand cups the area.

That is what love is.

Open. Unguarded. Complete.

Our lives have been intertwined before my birth, we've had our ups and downs, but it's all been worth it to end right in this moment.

My Beast. My King. My Savior.

I love you.

SERIES ORDER:
LITTLE LIES
LITTLE MATE
HALF TRUTHS: THEN
HALF TRUTHS: NOW
OMISSION PART ONE
OMISSION PART TWO

SPIN-OFFS:
COME TO ME
THE HUNT

The Beautiful Sinner Series are all interconnected standalones full of suspense and romance and an OTT alpha willing to burn the world to the ground for the woman he loves! It's sexy and has an edge of darkness that will leave you breathless! #MAFIAROMANCE

Now Live!
SIN #1
COVET #2
MINE #3
YOURS #4
RISQUE #5
OWN #6

Beautiful Sinner Spin-Off:
CORRUPT
MY SINFUL VALENTINE
SAVAGE KISS
ONE RULE

ABOUT THE AUTHOR

ELENA M. REYES IS THE EPITOME OF A FLORIDIAN AND IF SHE COULD
LIVE IN HER BELOVED FLIP-FLOPS, SHE WOULD.

As a small child, she was always intrigued by all forms of art:
whether it was dancing to island rhythms, or painting with any
medium she could get her hands on. Her passion for reading over the
years has amassed her with hours of pleasure, but it wasn't until she
stumbled upon fanfiction that her thirst to write overtook her world.

She's a short and sassy Latina with an adorable pup, a kiddo that
keeps her on her toes, and a husband who claims she'll cause him to
go bald prematurely. Lol

Want to keep up to date with Elena's crazy book life?

Follow here:

Website:
https://www.elenamreyes.com/

Find My Books Here:
https://www.bookbub.com/authors/elena-m-reyes

Email:
Reyes139ff@gmail.com

FB Reader Group:
Elena's Marked Girls. Come join the naughty fun.
Link: https://www.facebook.com/groups/1710869452526025/

facebook.com/AuthorElenaMReyes
x.com/ElenaMReyes
instagram.com/elenar139
amazon.com/Elena-M-Reyes/e/B00E3E26X8/ref=dp_byline_cont_pop_ebooks_1
bookbub.com/authors/elena-m-reyes
tiktok.com/@elenamreyes

<u>FATE'S BITE SERIES:</u>

LITTLE LIES
LITTLE MATE
HALF TRUTHS: THEN
HALF TRUTHS: NOW
OMISSION: PART ONE
OMISSION: PART TWO

<u>FATE'S BITE SPIN-OFFS:</u>

COME TO ME (2024)
THE HUNT (2024)

<u>BEAUTIFUL SINNER SERIES</u>

ALSO, BY ELENA M. REYES

Taste Of You
Doctor's Orders
Back To You

<u>STANDALONES:</u>

Craving Sugar
Stolen Kisses